"I Should Be The Father Of Your Baby," Jake Said.

Marisa realized her mouth was hanging open and closed it. "Are you sure about this?"

"It makes sense," he said. "You want to raise a child on your own—no husband or significant other, right?"

"Absolutely. But we're talking about creating a life, Jake—a baby. We're talking about sex. You and me, having sex. *Together*," Marisa said.

"Are you saying that you don't want to have sex with me? That you find me unappealing?"

"No! What woman wouldn't find you appealing?" Marisa leaned forward, clasping Jake's hands firmly between her own. "And I would be proud to carry your child. But you realize this isn't a one-shot deal. It could take months of trying," she said.

Jake nodded solemnly. "I'm in it for the long haul."

Dear Reader,

Welcome to Silhouette Desire and another month of sensual tales. Our compelling continuity DYNASTIES: THE DANFORTHS continues with the story of a lovely Danforth daughter whose well-being is threatened and the hot U.S. Navy SEAL assigned to protect her. Maureen Child's *Man Beneath the Uniform* gives new meaning to the term *sleepover!*

Other series this month include TEXAS CATTLEMAN'S CLUB: THE STOLEN BABY with Cindy Gerard's fabulous *Breathless for the Bachelor*. Seems this member of the Lone Star state's most exclusive club has it bad for his best friend's sister. Lucky lady! And Rochelle Alers launches a brand-new series, THE BLACKSTONES OF VIRGINIA, with *The Long Hot Summer,* which is set amid the fascinating world of horse-breeding.

Anne Marie Winston singes the pages with her steamy almost-marriage-of-convenience story, *The Marriage Ultimatum.* And in *Cherokee Stranger* by Sheri WhiteFeather, a man gets a second chance with a woman who wants him for her first time. Finally, welcome brand-new author Michelle Celmer with *Playing by the Baby Rules,* the story of a woman desperate for a baby and the hunky man who steps up to give her exactly what she wants.

Here's hoping Silhouette Desire delivers exactly what *you* desire in a powerful, passionate and provocative read!

Best,

Melissa Jeglinski

Melissa Jeglinski
Senior Editor, Silhouette Desire

Please address questions and book requests to:
Silhouette Reader Service
U.S.: 3010 Walden Ave., P.O. Box 1325, Buffalo, NY 14269
Canadian: P.O. Box 609, Fort Erie, Ont. L2A 5X3

Playing by the Baby Rules

MICHELLE CELMER

Silhouette® Desire

Published by Silhouette Books

America's Publisher of Contemporary Romance

SILHOUETTE BOOKS

ISBN 0-373-76566-5

PLAYING BY THE BABY RULES

This edition published by arrangement with Harlequin Books S.A.

® and TM are trademarks of Harlequin Books S.A., used under license.
Trademarks indicated with ® are registered in the United States Patent
and Trademark Office, the Canadian Trade Marks Office and in other
countries.

Visit Silhouette at www.eHarlequin.com

Printed in U.S.A.

MICHELLE CELMER

lives in southeastern Michigan with her husband, Steve, their three children, two dogs, two cats and a leopard gecko. When she's not writing or busy being a mom, you can find her in the garden weeding or curled up with a book. And if you twist her arm real hard you can usually persuade her into a day of power shopping.

Michelle loves to hear from readers. Visit her Web site at: www.michellecelmer.com.

To Steve for his unconditional support, and my children
for always being proud of me.

To my parents, who never doubted I would make it.

To Debby, Tonya, Jodi and all the Survivor ladies
for your invaluable critiques, and encouragement,
when it seemed hopeless.

And to Therese: There you have it....

One

"**I**'m telling you, Risa, all you need is a turkey baster."

Marisa Donato looked up from the new shipment of jasmine-scented aromatherapy candles she'd been shelving and shot Lucy Lopez, her moderately demented sales associate, a look of disgust. "Impregnate myself with a *turkey baster?* Tell me you're joking."

"I just figured, if you're so opposed to the idea of sex, why not?"

Marisa cringed as a pair of young women browsing near the push-up bras exchanged curious glances. Open talk of sex was probably common when the shop specialized in adult toys and pornographic videos. Since Marisa had transformed the store into Intimate Secrets, an upscale lingerie boutique, blatantly sexual merchandise was a thing of the past. Lucy's blatantly sexual language, however, was a habit Marisa hadn't yet broken.

Marisa lowered her voice. "I am not opposed to sex. Just that *kind* of sex. And even if I were to consider impregnating myself with a kitchen gadget, which I wouldn't in a million years, where am I going to get the, uh…genetic material?"

Oblivious to the customers, Lucy shrugged and said loudly, "I don't know. A sperm bank?"

She was rewarded with a round of giggles from the back of the store.

Marisa dropped her voice to a whisper. "I don't think you can just walk in and say, 'Hi, I'd like to make a withdrawal.' Besides, the whole idea is too weird."

"Okay, so the turkey baster is out." Lucy chose a candle from the stock behind the counter and dug a lighter out of her jeans pocket. She lit it, and the spicy sweet scent of cinnamon drifted up in a curl of smoke. "Why don't you just stick with your original plan and have it done artificially?"

"The doctor said the chances of the artificial insemination working are only ten to fifteen percent per cycle, and he's supposed to be one of the best fertility specialists in Michigan. With success rates like that, it could cost me a small fortune. He recommended doing it naturally."

"So you either find a small fortune or do it the old-fashioned way?"

"Exactly. And because of the endometriosis, it could take months to conceive."

Lucy leaned back, resting her elbows on the counter. "What you need is a man who would agree to unadulterated, no-strings-attached sex."

"More or less." The thought made her stomach

pitch. Ironically, her mother would have jumped at the offer. Make it a different man every night and she would have been in her glory.

"My God, Risa, what man wouldn't agree to that? There has to be a couple hundred in Royal Oak alone who would jump at the chance."

That's what she was afraid of. The idea of meaningless sex with some stranger just seemed so…*sleazy*. Unfortunately she was running out of options—and time.

What had begun as severe monthly cramping in her early teens was now relentless, stabbing pain. An annual checkup with her gynecologist revealed what she had already suspected. Radical surgery was inevitable. If she was going to have a baby, she was going to have to do it soon.

Artificial means had appeared to be the answer, until she'd learned the exorbitant fees and dismal success rates. Foreign and private adoptions were also far too pricey and domestic adoption for a middle-class, single working woman was practically unheard-of.

There was always the conventional "get married and have a family" routine. Collectively, her parents' eight divorces had taught her one important lesson—marital bliss didn't run in the family. By the time she left for college she'd lost track of how many "uncles" had come to stay with her and her mother. Uncles who, after Marisa had begun to develop physically, leered at her in a way that made her skin crawl. She hadn't dared sleep at night without a chair hooked under her doorknob. Just in case.

She would have given up on the prospect of children altogether, but lately, every time she passed a mother walking her baby in a stroller or pushing her toddler on the swings in the park, that twinge of envy she usually felt had turned into a dull, hollow ache. She longed to feel the unconditional love only a child could give, to share all of the love she'd stored up in her heart.

But sex with a stranger? Could she stoop so low when she'd deliberately spent her entire adult life avoiding that type of shallow existence?

"I don't know if I could do that," she told Lucy. "And if I did, it would have to be someone I would want to have sex with, and even more importantly, would want to procreate with."

"There has to be someone." Lucy blew a spiral of springy red hair out of her eyes. "Give me an idea of what you would be looking for."

Gathering her long gauzy skirt, Marisa settled on the stool behind the register and propped her elbows on the glass-top display case. "Well, first and foremost, he would have to be healthy—no weird genetic diseases running in his family."

"That's reasonable. You just ask for a family history. What else?"

"He would have to be attractive. Not necessarily gorgeous, although that would be a definite plus, but reasonably good-looking. And he would have to be nice. I couldn't have meaningless sex with someone I didn't like."

"That doesn't sound so hard." She counted off on her fingers. "Cute, nice and healthy—who do we know that fits that description?"

The bells above the front door chimed and Marisa opened her mouth to greet the customer entering the store, then realized it wasn't a customer. It was her best friend, Jake. He was slightly disheveled from the mid-July heat, wearing a rumpled Hawaiian-print shirt, cargo shorts and sandals.

When he saw them standing there, he broke into a wide grin. "Hey guys, what's up?"

Marisa looked at Lucy, and Lucy looked at her, then they both turned and looked at Jake again.

"Risa?" Lucy said, her unspoken question more than clear.

Her and Jake? Yeah, right. The idea was nearly as preposterous as the turkey baster. They had been best buddies since the fifth grade. Sure, she'd had a hopeless crush on him at first. *Every* girl in school had a crush on big, bad Jake Carmichael at one time or another. It was a teenage rite of passage.

But she wasn't a kid anymore. She would never risk damaging their friendship. It was far too important to her.

Marisa shook her head. "Absolutely not."

Jake stopped, absently rubbing his hand across a two-day-old beard the color of golden sand. "Why are you looking at me like that?"

"Like what?" she asked, pasting a smile on her face. "I thought you would be in the studio all afternoon."

"I needed a break." He nodded toward the door. "I've got sandwiches in the Jeep. I thought you might want to do lunch in the park."

"What a *nice* idea," Lucy said, turning to Marisa. "Isn't he a *nice* guy?"

"Yes, Lucy, he's very nice." Her eyes conveyed a silent warning—*zip it.*

Unfortunately, Lucy was never one to pick up on subtlety. "And you're looking very handsome today, Jake."

He looked down at his wrinkled clothes, raking a hand through his spiky, sun-streaked hair. "I am?"

She nodded. "Oh, definitely. And healthy. I'll bet

you don't have any weird genetic diseases in your family.''

Under the counter, Marisa planted the toe of one canvas shoe firmly in Lucy's shin as she smiled up at Jake. ''Why don't you grab the sandwiches and I'll meet you outside in a minute.''

He looked at them both kind of funny, then shrugged. ''Okay. I'm parked right down the street.''

The door had barely closed when Lucy opened her mouth to speak.

''*No,*'' Marisa interjected. ''Don't even suggest it.''

''Why not? He would be perfect! How you can be best friends with that man and not want to jump him on a daily basis is beyond me.''

Hopping down from her perch on the stool, Marisa grabbed her cell phone from her purse under the counter and slipped it into her skirt pocket. ''We don't have that kind of relationship.''

''Why not?''

''Because we *don't.* And this whole idea of finding some stranger to impregnate me is repulsive. I just can't do it, Luce. We'll have to think of something else.''

The browsing women appeared at the counter.

''Was that Jake Carmichael, the saxophone player?'' one of them asked, dropping a hot pink demi-bra on the counter.

Groupies. Ugh.

''The one and only,'' Marisa said, holding back a groan as she rang up her purchase.

The woman jabbed her friend and they both giggled. ''I told you it was him! He's *so* cute!''

Marisa resisted the urge to roll her eyes. ''Would you like a bottle of essential oil or a scented candle to go with that?''

"I've seen you at the bar when his band plays," the other girl said. "You're always up front. Is he like, your boyfriend?"

"Well, we really shouldn't say anything…." Lucy trailed off cryptically, nudging Marisa with her elbow. "It's not official yet."

"We won't tell anyone." The girl buying the bra turned to her friend. "Will we?"

Her friend shook her head enthusiastically. "Oh no, we won't tell a soul. Promise."

"Well, I guess if you promise not to tell…" Lucy leaned forward, lowering her voice. "They're engaged. They're planning a spring wedding."

"Really?" Bra-girl asked, looking heartbroken. "You're so lucky. He is *so* hot!"

Marisa smiled at the girls. "I'll be sure to tell him two of his biggest fans were in today. He'll appreciate the compliments." *Not.* Despite his rising popularity, he considered himself the same old Jake. The hero-worship garbage made him squirm.

"Maybe you could introduce us sometime," Bra-girl piped up. "We could, like, get his autograph or something."

"How about a lock of his hair," Lucy muttered under her breath.

Marisa bit down on the inside of her cheek to keep from laughing. "I'm sure we could arrange that," she said as she wrapped the bra in pink tissue paper and slipped it into a bag. "Come again, ladies."

As they walked away giggling, Lucy made a sound of disgust. "God, I detest groupies. They are fun to mess with though."

"I know, but I wish you wouldn't do that."

"What's the harm? It's all in good fun. Now, back to this sex thing—"

"No." Marisa shook her head. "We're definitely not getting back to the sex thing."

"Aw, come on—"

"*No*. I'll be back in a little while." She walked to the door and yanked it open. A suffocating wall of humidity and heat enveloped her. "Call me on my cell if you get swamped."

"Think about it," Lucy called after her. "Jake would be perfect!"

Flinging herself out the door, Marisa saw only a flash of color before promptly colliding face first into a very wide and very solid male chest.

"Whoa!" Jake caught her arm. "What's the rush."

The door swung shut, bumping her on the behind and knocking her even farther into him. She braced her hands against his chest to steady herself, instantly aware of the play of muscles beneath the sweat-moistened cotton shirt, the heat radiating from his skin. The sudden images racing through her mind, like exactly what she and Jake would have to do to make a baby, sent a funny little shiver down her spine. She never thought about stuff like that—least of all with Jake. It was all Lucy's fault for suggesting that she and Jake should—

No, they definitely shouldn't.

"What am I perfect for?" he asked.

He'd *heard* that? "Um…"

Jake stood, fingers still clasped firmly around her arm. His hands were large and strong but exceedingly gentle, his fingers long and graceful. It took a full five seconds to register the heat seeping through her blouse where he grasped her, and the hum of sensation traveling up her arm. She had to force herself not to jerk away.

"Earth to Marisa. You okay?"

She realized they were just standing there on the sidewalk, interrupting the heavy flow of afternoon foot traffic. Aware, too, that more than her arm had begun to tingle now, she gently extracted herself from his grasp. "I'm fine. Let's go."

"What am I perfect for?" he asked again as they started down Main Street on foot toward the park.

"It was nothing." Sweat began to soak the underside of her bra. It had to be about a million degrees out, which still didn't account for the heat creeping up into her face. There was no doubt in Marisa's mind, Lucy had done this on purpose. If she had just kept her mouth shut—

"After seventeen years, don't you think I can tell when you're lying." Jake poked her playfully. "Come on, tell me."

She shook her head. "You don't want to know."

"Sure I do."

"Trust me, you don't."

"Marisa, are you blushing?"

Jeez, couldn't he just drop it? "We should hurry, before someone gets our favorite spot." She walked faster, until she was almost jogging. Considering he was nearly a foot taller, he didn't have any trouble keeping up, and she was in danger of collapsing from heatstroke.

"I'm not going to stop asking, so you might as well spill it."

"I can't."

He batted obscenely long lashes at her—lashes any woman would kill for. "Please?"

"Nope."

"Pretty please? With sugar on top?" He was grinning down at her, his expression complete mischief. She had no doubt that he would relentlessly nag and harass her until she gave in.

He nudged her again. "C'mon, tell me. What am I perfect for?"

"*Sex*, Jake," she blurted out. "She thinks you're perfect for sex."

Two

Sex?

Jake walked beside Marisa to the park in stunned silence. Lucy thought he would be perfect for sex? That was...whoa. He wasn't quite sure how he was supposed to respond. He didn't want to hurt her feelings, but Marisa knew he didn't do relationships. Unless a relationship wasn't what Lucy had in mind.

"I warned you," Marisa said, her cheeks two hot pink smudges against a smooth olive complexion. "But you just had to know."

She'd warned him, and as usual, she was right. Once again he had let curiosity get the best of him. One of these days he would learn not to stick his nose into other people's business. How many times as a child had his curious nature gotten him several sound whacks from the old man's belt, or a crack across the jaw from the back of his hand?

They reached the park and automatically walked to the oak tree next to the fountain. Beneath a canopy of gnarled branches and dense green leaves, he spread the blanket on the grass and set the cooler down. He tugged his shirt over his head, rolled it into a makeshift pillow, and sprawled out on his back.

Marisa kicked off her sandals and sat down next to him, tossing her long, chestnut hair over her shoulder and tucking her knees under her chin. "Well, aren't you going to say something?"

Lucy—sex. Right. He propped himself up on his elbows. "Um, I don't know what to say."

A deep crease set in the middle of Marisa's brow—her disappointed face. Damn. He didn't want to hurt her feelings, but, *Lucy?*

"Lucy is nice, and I know you two are good friends, but…" He shrugged. "She's not really my type."

"Lucy?" The crease in her brow deepened, and for a second she looked as confused as he was feeling, then she started to laugh. Her laugh was full and rich and musical—like a symphony. He loved making her laugh, seeing her happy. Though, it would have been nice to know *why* she was laughing.

"Feel like letting me in on the joke?"

"You think I want you to go out with Lucy?"

Now he was totally confused. "Don't you?"

She laughed harder, her eyes overflowing with tears. "Don't worry, Jake. Lucy doesn't want to go out with you. She was speaking hypothetically."

"Oh. Well, I'm flattered, I guess." What he really wanted to know, but would never ask, was what did Marisa think? And why had they been talking about *him* in the first place? Would Marisa ever consider him…?

No. He dismissed the idea before it could evolve into

something stronger, like hope. He'd learned not to hope for things that were never meant to be. Especially not that.

Everyone had a destiny, and for him, a family just wasn't in the cards. He would hurt them, then he would have to spend the rest of his life regretting it. Maybe if things were different.

But things weren't different. They never would be, and every now and then he had to remind himself of that.

Rolling onto his stomach, he opened the cooler and unpacked the sandwiches, potato chips and diet sodas he'd picked up at the deli on Fourth Street. "Chicken salad or tuna?"

"You know, you shouldn't run around half-naked," Marisa said, taking the chicken salad. "It's embarrassing. You're giving every female in the park a hot flash."

He looked around, noticed several pairs of female eyes glued in his direction, then turned back to Marisa, who was picking onions off her sandwich and tossing them onto the grass. Not every female.

He reached over and tugged on the sleeve of her blouse, wondering how she didn't melt in the blistering heat covered from head to toe in yards of fabric. For reasons he'd never understood, she hid her voluptuous curves behind loose draping clothes. "I'll put some clothes on if you take some off."

She gave him an eye roll. "You're very funny."

"I'm serious, Marisa. You have a nice figure. Why do you always keep it covered?"

"Trust me, if you looked like this, you'd keep it covered too."

"You know, lots of men like voluptuous women."

Do you like voluptuous women? The question balanced on the tip of her tongue, but she bit it back. One, because she knew he preferred his women tall, blond and waify—the antithesis to her own short, dark and curvy—and two, because it didn't matter one way or the other. He was her best friend, her buddy. He didn't find her attractive in that way.

"Maybe I just don't like the kind of men who would like a woman like that," she said. She knew exactly the kind of men who liked a woman like her—the kind who wanted only one thing from a voluptuous body. The kind of men her mother used to drag home from the bar. The kind of men who, when they tired of her mother, turned their attention to Marisa. A teenager. Though none had even tried anything physical, their leering eyes had been enough to make her feel violated and defiled. Dirty.

Maybe her mother could live that way, but Marisa knew she could never be that kind of woman—not for *any* reason.

Across the park, she heard the delighted squeals of children playing. She forced herself not to look, for fear that her heart would break. For her, there would be no meaningless sex with a stranger. She could never live with herself. She would have to accept that, until she could afford some artificial means of impregnation or foreign adoption, there would be no children in her life. And if she were never able to afford it, or it took too long, she would have to accept that motherhood for her wasn't meant to be.

The possibility felt like a knife in her chest, and for a moment she thought for sure that her heart *was* breaking.

"Marisa? Hey, are you crying?"

Reaching up, she touched her cheek and was surprised to find that it was damp. What was wrong with her? Embarrassed, she sniffled and wiped her face with the back of her hand.

Jake sat up next to her. "God, I'm sorry. I was just kidding. I didn't mean to hurt your feelings."

"Jake, it wasn't you. I've just got a lot on my mind today. You know, baby stuff."

He smacked his forehead. "The fertility specialist. I completely forgot about your appointment. What did he say?"

"It's not looking like it's going to happen anytime soon. If ever." Fresh tears rolled down her cheeks and she brushed them away, forcing a smile. "Just ignore me."

Jake had learned from years of experience that solitude was the last thing Marisa wanted or needed at a time like this. She had the unhealthy habit of letting things eat away at her until a total emotional meltdown was inevitable. It looked like this would be one for the record books.

"Com'ere," he said.

She looked up at him, her deep brown eyes full of pain. Her lower lip quivered as she bravely fought her tears. "I'm okay, really."

"No, you're not. I know how much having a baby means to you." Shifting closer, he tugged her toward him. It was all the coercing she needed to dissolve into his arms. He held her, stroking her hair as a river of her tears, intermingled with his sweat, rolled down his bare chest to the waist of his pants. The sensation was almost…erotic.

Erotic? He instantly felt like a slime. She needed comfort—a shoulder to cry on. Impure thoughts involving Marisa had been excusable back in middle school when his hormones had been raging and her breasts had just begun developing. Since then, he'd managed to keep those urges in check. For the most part, at least. Every now and then he indulged in a little fantasy, like finding out what she was hiding under all of those clothes. She owned a lingerie shop. It just stood to reason that she wore sexy underthings. He could imagine her in lace—red lace. Or better yet, black.

A sudden and intense tug of arousal stole his breath. Now was definitely not the time to be thinking about black lace. Especially when it pertained to Marisa's body. It was just that he'd never felt the caress of her hands on his bare back, or noticed how sweet her hair smelled, or how soft it felt against his cheek.

Maybe he'd just never felt the lush swell of her breasts—

Whoa, stop right there. He was *not* going to start thinking about her breasts. Though he had to admit that it was tough to ignore them when they pillowed so softly against him. And he realized suddenly, that his hands were straying lower, gently caressing her through her blouse, exploring places they shouldn't be.

She chose that moment to pull back and dig a tissue out of her pocket. "I'm really sorry about this," she said, wiping her nose. She gave him a shaky smile, tears still clinging to her long, dark lashes. "I guess I needed to vent."

"Vent on me anytime," he said. "That's what I'm here for."

"Oh, jeez, I got you all wet." She pulled a fresh tissue out and wiped the moisture from his shoulder and chest. Sliding lower, closer to his waist, her fingers brushed against the taut skin of his stomach and a stab of desire pierced his gut. Instinctively he jerked.

She looked at him strangely, then, as if realizing what she'd done, her eyes widened and she yanked her hand back. "Sorry."

There was a brief, awkward silence then her lower lip began to tremble and fresh tears rolled down her cheeks.

It broke his heart to see her so miserable. If anyone deserved unconditional happiness, it was Marisa.

Abandoning any inappropriate thoughts, he pulled her into his arms. "I'm so sorry, Marisa. Is there anything I can do to help?"

You could have sex with me. Marisa wondered what his reaction would be if she were to blurt it out. Would he be appalled? Intrigued? Would he fall back on the blanket laughing hysterically?

Probably the latter. There was no use speculating, because it would never happen. She would never work up the nerve to ask. She would never be able to handle the rejection when she heard that inevitable no.

"It comes down to me not having enough money saved," she said, sniffling and resting her cheek against his damp shoulder. "I considered mortgaging the shop to make up the difference, but if I'm going to have a baby, I don't want to jeopardize my financial security."

"If I could, I would lend you the money, but producing this CD is sucking up all of my cash. I've had people calling me constantly with studio work, so much I've had to turn some of it down, but things are still tight."

"I'll get over this—eventually."

Jake's arms tightened around her. She felt the tickle of his breath against her hair, smelled the balmy scent of the spearmint candies he bought by the case since he'd given up cigarettes. Was it just her imagination or had they been touching each other an awful lot today? Or maybe they had always touched each other and it just felt different now. Not just different, but...nice.

Too nice.

"What really sucks," he said, "is that if we pooled our money together, we could probably do one or the other, but that would mean one of us would have to sacrifice."

"I could still get pregnant," she said. "I would just have to find a man to—" She realized her mistake the second the words were out, but it was too late to take them back.

The hand that had been gently rubbing her shoulder came to a dead stop. "Find a man to do what, Marisa?"

There was a long, silent pause. Marisa extracted herself from Jake's arms and glanced down at her wrist. "Wow, will you look at the time."

Jake noted with amusement that she wasn't wearing a watch. "Where are you going?"

"I should head back to the shop. Lucy probably needs me."

As Jake watched her hastily rewrap her untouched sandwich and stuff it into the cooler, everything began to make a weird sort of sense. "When I walked into the store today, what were you and Lucy talking about?"

She avoided his eyes. "You know. The sex thing."

"But *why* were you talking about it?"

"No reason." She started to get up, but he reached for her arm and tugged her back down.

"You're blushing again," he said.

She reached up and pressed her fingers to her cheek.

"Were you talking about getting pregnant when I walked in?" he asked.

Sinking her teeth into her bottom lip, she nodded.

Holy—

Jake's heart began to race. He could hardly choke out the next question. "Is that what Lucy meant when she said I would be perfect?"

He could barely believe it when her head wobbled up and down. He dropped her arm and sat back, stunned. Him getting Marisa pregnant? Lucy thought he would be perfect, but what did Marisa think? What did *he* think?

There was one obvious advantage to the situation— sex with Marisa. That alone would be tough to pass up. But he'd decided a long time ago that he would never have a family. He would be a lousy father, and an equally lousy husband. But Marisa wasn't looking for a family, he reminded himself. She just wanted a baby.

His baby?

"I know." Marisa laughed nervously. "I told Lucy what a stupid idea it is. I mean, you and me having a baby? Yeah, right."

"Yeah, right," he agreed, equal parts disappointment and relief burning through him. Either she didn't think he was good enough to father her child, or the thought of making love to him was so repulsive she would never consider it.

No matter the reason, she was probably right. It was a crazy idea.

"So, you ready to go?" Marisa stood next to the blanket, cooler in hand. The sun burned bright behind her, hiding her face in shadow, but he could tell by her tone that she was anxious to leave. He'd lost his appetite anyway.

"Yeah, sure." He pulled his shirt on and balled up the blanket, tucking it under his arm. They were both quiet as they walked back to her shop. When they got there she handed him the cooler.

"This isn't going to make things weird, is it?" she asked, concern etched in the corners of her eyes. "You know, the whole baby thing."

If he let it, maybe. But he wasn't going to let himself take it personally. Nor could he blame her for thinking he wouldn't be the right man to father her child. After all, she knew him better than anyone.

"Do you know how many women have come up to me after a show and offered to have my children?" He gave her a playful nudge. "I'm used to it."

She handed him the cooler. "So, we're good?"

"Yeah, we're good."

She reached for the door handle, then stopped, turning back to him. "Because it would be kind of strange. You know, you and me...*together*."

He nodded. "Yep. Pretty strange."

"I mean, not *bad* strange. Just, different. It would change everything."

"It certainly would." Possibly for the better. Or possibly not. It was the *not* side of that coin that made him uneasy. Without Marisa, he wouldn't have anyone. He wasn't prepared to jeopardize their friendship.

"You're playing tonight?" Marisa asked.

"Nine-thirty. If you're planning on coming, I'll stop by and walk you down. It's on my way. We're trying out some new material tonight."

"Okay."

"So, that's a yes?"

"That's a yes." She pulled the door open, letting out a rush of cool dry air, then stopped again, turning back to him. She looked as if she might say something, then she shook her head and disappeared inside.

The bells over the door jingled softly as it swung shut, and he couldn't shake the feeling that, despite his assurances otherwise, things had changed anyway.

Three

———

"**R**isa, Jake's here," Lucy called from the front of the store. "Are you ready to go?"

Wincing as pain clutched low in her belly, Marisa shelved the day's receipts and stored the cash in the safe. "Go ahead and lock up. I'll be right out."

Jake poked his head around the corner. "Anything I can do?"

She wiped a trickle of sweat from her brow. "Nope, I'll be ready in just a second."

"Hey, you okay? You look a little pale."

She forced a smile. "Feminine stuff. I'll be fine."

He nodded, no more explanation necessary. It wouldn't be the first time he'd seen her in pain, and probably wouldn't be the last either. "If you're not feeling good, you don't have to come to the bar tonight."

"I'll be okay in a few minutes. Tell Lucy I'll be right out."

She grabbed a bottle of aspirin from the cabinet above the sink in the bathroom and chased three down with water. Clutching the edge of the sink, she sucked in several deep breaths while she waited for the spasms to cease. Every bout of pain lately was a grim reminder she was running out of time. She would only be able to take so much more before she had to give in and have the surgery.

"Risa," Lucy popped her head in. "Someone here to see you."

"Did you tell them we're closed?"

"I tried, but he said it's personal. Some guy and his daughter."

Some guy and his…oh no, it couldn't be. She closed her eyes, shaking her head. Please, not tonight, she prayed silently.

She followed Lucy to the front, and of course, it was him. He always managed to show up when she didn't want to see him. Which, come to think of it, was most of the time. How long had it been anyway? A year? Maybe longer?

Still tall and handsome, he looked a decade younger than his fifty-two years. The only hint of his true age was the distinguished trace of gray peppering his temples. The woman next to him was poured into a black-and-gold dress and clung to his arm. Maybe she was afraid of busting an ankle on her four-inch spiked heels.

"Marisa," he said stiffly, gazing with barely masked distaste around the store.

She told herself not to let the rejection bother her, but deep down it stung. There was still a remnant of the little girl in her that used to try so hard to please him.

"Hello, Joseph. Long time no see."

"I'd like to introduce you to Julia."

"It's so nice to finally meet you, Marisa. I've heard so much about you."

I'll bet you have, Marisa thought, accepting her petite hand. She knew Joseph had always preferred younger women, but this was obscene. She couldn't have been more than twenty.

Lucy stood next to her and appeared perplexed. Jake hovered near the counter looking as if he wanted to disappear.

"Where are my manners," she said. "Joseph, you remember my friend Jake, and this is Lucy Lopez. We work together. Lucy, this is Joseph Donato, my father."

Joseph gave them both a slight nod.

"So, when's the big day?" Marisa asked.

Julia looked up at him, confused. "You told her already?"

Marisa gestured to Julia's right hand. "The rock you're wearing tipped me off. How many does this make, Joseph? Five or six?"

A nerve twitched in his jaw, and he eyed her sternly. "You know very well that Melinda was my fourth wife, which will make Julia my fifth."

She challenged his piercing gaze. "You never know. I thought maybe you slipped one in somewhere without telling me."

"Marisa," Julia said, stepping forward. "Joey and I wanted to invite you to join us for dinner, to celebrate our engagement."

"Really?" She could barely hide her surprise. "Whose idea was that?"

Julia glanced nervously at Joseph. "Um, both of ours."

Boy, was she a lousy liar. Marisa knew Joseph wouldn't have voluntarily asked her to join him for a meal. Still, she had no reason to be rude to Julia. "I'm sorry, I have plans tonight. But thank you for the invitation."

"You will come to the wedding, won't you?"

She'd never attended one of her father's weddings. Well, not since his second marriage when her mother had sent her to the formal reception decked out in a ratty old dress and scuffed shoes. She had wanted all of his guests to see how poorly he cared for his daughter. She'd given no thought to how mortified Marisa would feel.

"Your father doesn't love you," her mother had said. "He only cares about himself, and now everyone will know it."

It never escaped Marisa's attention that her mother had a closet full of designer clothes and shoes. But when Marisa needed money for school clothes, or the rent was due, the well was always dry.

"It's August eighteenth," Julia was saying. "Can you make it?"

Marisa scrambled for an excuse to decline.

"It would mean so much to us," Julia pressed. The look she gave Marisa was nearly pleading. "Please come."

Pity for the girl overshadowed reason. Julia seemed nice enough. Clueless—but nice. "Sure, I'll come."

"Oh good!" she said excitedly. Joseph stood next to her, his face solemn. "I'll send you an invitation."

"We should go," Joseph said, taking her arm. "We'll miss our reservations."

"It was so nice meeting you." Julia took Marisa's hand again, this time squeezing it firmly. "I hope we see each other again soon."

Joseph nodded in her direction. "Take care of yourself, Marisa," he said, guiding Julia to the door.

"It was nice meeting you, too, Lucy and Jake!" Julia waved as the door jangled shut.

"Whoa." Lucy leaned against the counter next to Jake. "That was tense."

"Very tense," Jake agreed. "On a scale of one to ten, I'd give it a sphincter level of about ninety-nine point nine."

"Your father is gorgeous," Lucy said.

Marisa grabbed her purse from the file-cabinet drawer and pulled out her keys. "Don't think he doesn't know it."

Lucy switched the lights off and they started toward the door. "Are you really going to go to their wedding?"

"I might. I'm a little curious, I guess." They stepped outside into the stifling heat and Marisa locked up behind them.

"Your family is so scandalous," Lucy said. "I envy you. I've got a family full of practicing Catholics. It's so dull."

They wove their way down Main Street toward the bar. As was the case every Friday night, the streets of the trendy town were clogged with people. "Lucy, trust me when I tell you it's not as exciting as you may think. Especially for the people directly involved."

Jake only nodded silently. Having grown up in an

equally dysfunctional family, no one had to explain the concept to him.

When they reached the bar, they walked past the long line of customers waiting for a table and the bouncer motioned them through the door.

They negotiated through a sea of people to the table marked Reserved just to the left of the dance floor.

"I'll see you after the set," Jake said, and headed for the stage, instantly encompassed by the usual preperformance harem.

Having been so distracted by the pain and her father's unexpected visit, Marisa barely noticed Jake's appearance. Not that he looked any different than usual. Under the dim, smoky lights he looked unbelievably handsome. Well, actually, he looked unbelievably handsome all the time. And it wasn't just good looks that made him so attractive. There were endearing little things that added to his appeal. The hair that was always a little messy. The slightly crooked nose—a battle scar from one of his father's rages—and the way his mouth lifted a fraction higher on the left when he smiled.

He turned and flashed her that crooked grin and a funny little flutter danced through her stomach.

From across the table, Lucy nudged her.

She tore her eyes away from the stage. "Huh?"

"I said, Jake looks good tonight."

A rush of heat claimed her cheeks when she realized she'd been caught staring. She tried to sound casual. "Oh, yeah, I guess he does."

"You need a tissue?"

"What for?"

"The drool on your chin."

Before she could embarrass herself further with a de-

nial Lucy would most surely see right through, a waitress appeared to take their drink orders. A moment later
Jake introduced the band and began the set with a rich,
lazy rhythm, rendering a hush over the entire bar. Marisa propped her chin on the back of her hands, gazing
up at him, lulled by a haunting tune she didn't recognize. Then he sought her out, his eyes locking on hers,
and she had the irrational, almost thrilling sensation that
they were the only two people there. That he was playing for her alone. A slow, melodic seduction. She'd
never heard him play more soulfully.

It went on that way throughout the forty-minute set
and by the end, she felt as if she'd been picked apart,
dragged out emotionally and left raw and exposed.

A burst of wild applause snapped her back to reality.
His music had touched everyone there, not just her. Although, he had been watching her…

Jake thanked the crowd, passed the entertainment
over to the DJ, then eased his way past a throng of eager
young women. Between autographs and words of
praise, he slowly made his way to Marisa and Lucy's
table. As Marisa rose to greet him, a tall, leggy blonde
seated at the table behind them body-slammed her out
of the way. Marisa stumbled, catching her balance on
the edge of the table.

The blonde attached herself to Jake like a leech,
whispering in his ear. He laughed, whispered something
in return and when she handed him a business card he
tucked it into his shirt pocket. It occurred to Marisa that
Jake *hadn't* been looking at her.

He'd been fixed on the blonde sitting directly behind
her.

Humiliation blistered Marisa's pride. What had she

been thinking? Why would she let herself believe that Jake could look at her as anything but a friend? How could she have ever even considered that he would agree to be her baby's father? That the thought of making love to her might not be such a bad thing after all. She should have known better.

Though she wanted to deny it, something had happened between them today. Something had changed and she didn't know how to reverse it. How to fix it.

"Sorry about that." Jake folded himself into the chair opposite her and signaled the waitress for his usual soda. "The longer I'm in this business, the more aggressive they seem to get."

"Poor baby," Lucy teased, and he pinched her playfully, making her squeal.

Holding in the tears of humiliation burning behind her eyes, Marisa grabbed her purse and rose from her chair. "I'm going home."

"Already?" Disappointment twisted Jake's gut. He had hoped she would stay for a while, so he could see if the connection he'd experienced, the charge of electricity he'd felt pass between them, was real or a figment of his imagination. "You're sure you can't stay a while?"

"I'm beat."

"Do you mind if I stay?" Lucy asked. "Or do you want company walking home?"

"You should stay," Marisa told her. "Have a good time."

Jake got up. "I'll walk you home."

"You don't have to do that."

"I don't like you walking home alone at night. See you later, Luce."

"You two have fun," Lucy called after them. Her tone suggested she knew exactly what had been on Jake's mind all night. Hell, all day. As hard as he tried, he just couldn't shake it.

On the way out he saw the producer who'd approached him. She appeared deep in conversation with the owner of the bar, but as he passed, she glanced over and mouthed the words *call me*.

He'd tried to explain that he was producing his music himself, under an independent label, but she wouldn't take no for an answer. He was approached regularly by so-called producers. He'd gone that route before. Never again would he sign away his creative rights. This was *his* music. He would record it the way he saw fit. Though he made a decent living as a studio musician, and he enjoyed the work, writing music was his true passion.

The night air was still heavy with moisture as they stepped out the door, but the temperature had lowered to a semitolerable level. A warm breeze carried the rich scent of coffee from the shop two doors down, and cars, spitting exhaust and overflowing with rowdy teenagers, lined the narrow city streets.

Jake draped one arm loosely across Marisa's shoulder as they walked down the street together. They'd walked this way countless times before, but tonight was different. Tonight he was hyperaware of her presence beside him. The softness of her hair brushing against his arm, the scent of her perfume tantalizing his nose, the occasional bump of her hip against his thigh as they walked.

Marisa, however didn't seem to notice a thing. She

stared off, oblivious to his presence, her mind a million miles away.

"What did you think of the set?" he asked, curious to know if she'd felt anything special. Anything different.

"It was good," she said noncommittally. "I like the new material."

Disappointment took a choke hold on his heart. Okay, so she hadn't felt it. She probably hadn't even been looking at him, just staring blindly into space, thinking about the store inventory or shampooing her hair. Why would he let himself think—believe—it could have been anything else?

He'd promised he wouldn't let what happened this afternoon compromise their friendship, and here he was flaking out. But he couldn't seem to erase the idea from his mind. He'd run the situation over in his head a thousand times today and still one question nagged him.

Could he bring a child into the world, his own flesh and blood, then give it up?

Then it had dawned on him. He wouldn't really be giving it up. As Marisa's friend, he would always be a part of the kid's life, but distanced enough to keep from doing any irreparable damage. It would be sort of like having a family, without really having one.

He could take the kid to the zoo, or teach him to play baseball. The little guy would never have to know the truth. At least, not until he was older. Even then he would probably be better off not knowing what kind of family he'd come from. What kid would want to learn he'd had an abusive, alcoholic grandfather and an uncle serving a life sentence in prison? It just wouldn't be fair to burden a kid with that.

Hell, he could even start a college fund and, of course, if Marisa ever needed support financially, or just someone to baby-sit, he would be there for her. He could teach him about music—start him early learning the fundamentals. If someone had bothered to take the time with Jake, had recognized his musical potential, who knows where he would be today. Marisa's kid would have the best of everything.

The more he'd thought about it, the more he liked the idea. Somehow the concept of her raising his child just felt right.

He'd tried to dismiss it. He'd tried to ignore the voice inside telling him it would be the right thing to do, that he owed it to Marisa for all she'd done for him. For being his best friend. His only family.

But he hadn't been able to shut the voice out. The big question was, would Marisa go for it? Would she think he was good enough?

"I was wondering," Marisa said, breaking the silence. "How would you feel about coming to the wedding with me. I could use the moral support."

He understood completely. "Sure, I'll go."

When they reached her building, she stopped and pulled out her keys. "Thanks for walking me home. Do you want to come up for a bit?"

He shoved his hands into his pants pockets, suddenly filled with nervous energy. This was his chance. He forced the words out. "Sure. I kinda wanted to talk to you about something, anyway."

"Okay." Marisa started up the stairs to her apartment above the shop. As they stopped in the hall outside her door, the door to the adjacent apartment opened a crack, snapping tightly against half-a-dozen security chains. A single eyeball peered out.

"It's just us, Mr. Kloppman," she called. "Marisa and Jake."

"Hand please," a muffled voice ordered, and a small metal cheese grater slid through the opening. Obediently Marisa held out her hand and the grater hovered briefly over her palm. "Next."

Jake did the same. When Mr. Kloppman appeared confident they were who they claimed to be, he slid the chains free and opened the door.

"Can't be too careful," he said, his eyes shifting nervously up and down the short hallway. "I saw it on the news. They can change shape, look or sound like anyone."

Behind her, Jake chuckled and Marisa elbowed him sharply in the gut. "Have you been watching *X-Files* again, Mr. Kloppman?"

He shook his head. "Heck no. This was on the late news last night. You keep your doors locked. It's not safe." He backed into his apartment, again checking the short stretch of the hallway. "Trust no one," he said as the door snapped shut.

"That guy is certifiable," Jake said, after they were safely inside her apartment with the door locked. "I'm afraid he's going to snap one of these days and hurt someone."

"He's harmless. Besides, his daughter pays the rent on time every month and as long as he lives next door I never have to worry about an alarm system." Clearing a week's worth of newspapers off the couch, Marisa collapsed onto the overstuffed cushions, stretching out her legs. "So, what did you want to talk to me about?"

Jake sat across from her in the leather recliner and leaned forward, hands clasped between his knees. "It's about what happened today at lunch."

Marisa's heart began to hammer wildly in her chest. "I've been thinking about that, too."

"It's pretty much the *only* thing I've been thinking about. How about you?"

"Me, too."

"Is it just me, or do you get the feeling that somehow the dynamics of our entire relationship have changed?"

She didn't want things to change, but she couldn't deny that something was different. Looking down at her hands, she nodded.

"In that case, I think Lucy is right," he said. "I should be the father of your baby."

Four

Marisa's head snapped up. "I beg your pardon?"

"I've been thinking about it all day, and I've come to the conclusion that I would be the perfect man to father your child."

She realized her mouth was hanging open and closed it. The idea of having Jake's baby had been funny when Lucy suggested it. Funny in a "yeah, like that would ever happen" way. But this was Jake suggesting it, looking at her as if…as if he was seriously *considering* it.

"Are you sure about this?"

"Think about it," he said. "What was the main reason we decided it would be a bad idea? We were afraid things would get weird. That we would feel differently about our relationship. But that's already happened."

He had a point. She did feel different, and as much as she'd like to believe otherwise, with the progression of her condition, this could be her last chance to have a baby.

"Look," he said, "you want to raise a child on your own, no husband or significant other, right?"

"Absolutely."

"I don't want a wife and kids—ever. You're not going to find too many men willing to permanently give up their parental rights. But you know me. You can trust me."

"I don't doubt that you would honor any agreement we made. But you're talking about creating a life, Jake—a baby. You do understand that?"

"Of course I do. You would be an amazing mother, Marisa. You deserve that chance."

"Maybe I'm not making myself clear. We're talking about *sex*. You and me, having sex. *Together*."

"Are you trying to say that you wouldn't want to have sex with me? That you find me unappealing?"

"No! No, it's not that at all. Jeez, what woman wouldn't find you appealing?"

"As far as the gene pool goes, I know I don't come from the best stock—"

"Your genes are just fine." She leaned forward, clasping his hands firmly between her own. "I would be proud to carry your child. My biggest fear—my only fear—is that it might damage our friendship."

"You're my dearest friend, nothing could ever change that."

She'd never seen him look so serious, so sincere. He made it sound simple—have sex, make a baby.

Maybe it sounded *too* simple.

"You realize that this isn't necessarily a one-shot deal. It could take months," she said. "A year even. If it happens at all."

He nodded solemnly. "I understand. I'm in it for the long haul."

"And we would have to establish some ground rules. So things don't get…confusing. Because things could get awfully confusing, Jake. This is going to change everything."

"I think setting rules is a good idea."

"Can you promise me that, no matter what, this will not damage our friendship? You can handle this?"

"I can handle it. I promise." He squeezed her hands. "I *want* to do this for you."

He could handle it, but could she? She knew she should take her time, think this over for a while. She also knew deep in her heart the decision was already made. There had never been a doubt.

"Okay," she agreed. "Let's do it."

Marisa set her wine on the coffee table, dug a legal pad from under a pile of newspapers and pulled a purple gel pen from between the couch cushions. "Are you ready?"

Jake nodded. "Can I take the first one?"

She marked a big purple *One* on the first line, noting that her hands had finally stopped shaking but her stomach was still a maze of tightly bound knots. Excitement, nerves, fear—she couldn't recall ever feeling so many intense emotions all at once.

"I say that we have to be totally honest with each other at all times if this is going to work. Even about things that might make us uncomfortable."

"Okay, rule number one—total honesty. And I think our number two rule should be that we only, um…do it—"

"Time out." He held his hands up in a tee shape.

"Before we go any further, we should establish what it is we're going to be doing."

She arched a brow at him. "Let me guess, you missed that chapter in Health class?"

He leaned forward and swatted her foot playfully. "Very funny. I meant, we should decide what to call it. Sex, doing it—there are dozens of ways to label it. I think we should pick one, and stick to it. To keep things consistent."

His relaxed attitude did little to ease her nerves. He seemed awfully open-minded about this. Almost too open-minded. Like he did this kind of thing all the time.

"What do *you* think we should call it?"

He rubbed his chin. "Well, to say that it's just sex seems a little cold considering our main objective. When you're holding your baby, and you look back on his or her conception, I want it to be with good feelings."

Her throat tightened and grateful tears burned behind her eyes. "That is so sweet."

He caught and held her gaze, his eyes gentle and full of understanding. "I want to do this right. I love you, and I like to think that you love me, too."

She plucked a tissue from a box on the coffee table and wiped her eyes. "You know I do."

"Then, I think we should say we're making love— if you're comfortable with that. Even though we're not *in love,* we do love each other. Right?"

"Okay, from now on it's making love."

"Settled," he said. "Back to rule number two."

"I think we should agree that we only, um, make love during the period of time that I'm ovulating. You know, since that's the only reason we're doing this."

He paused for a second, and she could swear she saw

a flash of disappointment. Then he nodded. "Yeah, that's probably a good idea."

"And rule number three, so it's consistent, we should establish where we make love, and number four, agree that afterward we go home. No sleepovers. Again, that could complicate things."

"Since it stands to reason that at some point we'll be making love at night, I think it should be here. I don't want you to have to worry about getting home afterward, and I'm just guessing about this, but you probably want to stay off your feet. So everything stays where it's supposed to."

"That's a good point. I never even considered that." She jotted it down. The next one was going to be tough. "Number five, and think good and hard about this one, because you could be looking at a year or more. No sleeping with anyone else while we're involved. It's not that I don't trust you, but with all the nasty diseases out there, I can't take any chances. We're going to be having a lot of unprotected sex."

"Can I date other women?"

She tried not to let the question sting. She'd been expecting it, especially after the incident in the bar tonight, and it was only fair. "I don't see why not. As long as you don't sleep with them."

With hardly any consideration, he nodded. "Okay. I can do that."

"You're *sure?*"

He looked hurt by her skepticism. "Of course I'm sure. I know everyone thinks I'm some superstud, but it's actually very rare that I take a woman to bed. And just so you know, when I do, I *always* use a condom— no exceptions."

"I believe you."

"And that brings us to the next rule. Keeping this to ourselves."

She had a sinking sensation in the pit of her stomach. He didn't want people to know they were sleeping together. That shouldn't have surprised her. After all, he had his superstud reputation to protect. It still hurt a little. "If you think that's best."

"Until you decide what you want to tell the kid when he's older, we should keep it quiet. In my business, these things have a way of getting around."

Shame burned her cheeks. Why did she automatically assume the worst? Here he was considering the best interests of the baby and she'd taken it as personal insult.

"At some point we will have to figure out how we want to handle that," she said. "You know, when he or she asks why Dad isn't around."

"That'll be phase two, after we actually get you pregnant."

"Fair enough. That puts us at number seven." She grabbed her wineglass and took a hearty swig. She hadn't said a word and already her cheeks were on fire. God, she hadn't blushed this much since she was twelve. "Um…"

"Total honesty," he reminded her.

"It's important that you don't…*pleasure* yourself for the two weeks before I ovulate. It's the only way to keep your sperm count up. The more sperm, the better chance I have of conceiving."

He winced. "Two weeks, huh?"

"It's what all of the literature on the subject says to do. Sorry."

"No, don't be sorry. I'll survive." He looked up at

her, his smile playful. "I don't suppose that same rule applies to you."

"Um, I don't know…"

Jake laughed. "Marisa, I was joking. If you want to make yourself feel good, go right ahead. Maybe, to make up for my torturous two weeks of celibacy, you'll let me watch you."

She opened her mouth to respond, but nothing came out. He had to be joking. He didn't really expect her to—

Oh my God, what if he did? Maybe he was used to that kind of thing.

"Marisa, *relax,* I was kidding."

She let out a shaky breath. "Sorry, I guess I'm just a little nervous about all of this."

"Don't be. We're good friends. We've done practically everything else together. Do you get nervous when we have a picnic in the park, or go see a movie?"

"Of course not."

"Then try to think of this as one more thing we're doing as friends."

Friends who have sex?

Well, she'd never had a friend like *that* before. What kind of sex did friends have, anyway? Going-through-the-motions, let's-get-this-over-with sex, or pulse-pounding, mind-blowing passionate sex? And suppose he *wanted* pulse-pounding sex, but she didn't know how to pleasure him? She didn't want him to be disappointed, or after two whole weeks of waiting walk away unsatisfied.

Worst of all, what if he looked at her body and was completely turned off?

Jake sat down next to her on the couch and draped an arm over her shoulder. She tried not to tighten every muscle in her body as the weight of his thigh pressed against her own and sent little tingles up and down her leg. He'd sat this close lots of times and it had never made her tingle before. Not in the past ten years, anyway.

No. She refused to let herself blow this out of proportion. Forcing herself to relax, she let her head drop on his shoulder. There, that was nice.

Hmm, *very* nice.

"Is that it?" he asked, taking the legal pad from her.

"I think we covered just about everything. We can always add to it later."

"We have seven rules. Maybe that's lucky."

Yeah, maybe they would get lucky and conceive in the first month. "Jake, I want you to know how much I appreciate this."

"I know you do." He squeezed her shoulder. "I think it's going to work out real well."

"Me, too."

"Although I do have just one more question."

"What's that?"

He looked down at her with a grin that could make a woman forget her own name. "When do we get started?"

Jake leaned over the console in the control room, wincing as his crotch bumped the hard metal edge.

He'd been daydreaming about Marisa again—more to the point, making love to Marisa. Since she'd begun testing for ovulation every afternoon, he'd thought about little else.

He'd imagined her in a slew of locations—the sofa, the kitchen counter, backstage at the club. He'd even pictured her sprawled on the control panel in the studio, wearing nothing but a smile. That was by far his favorite, and had landed him in his current condition.

He winced again as the throb in his groin reached a new, excruciating level. He hadn't fantasized this much since middle school, when physical pleasure—with another person at least—was still mysterious and new.

In reality, he sometimes went months without giving sex, in any form, much thought. Lately he was feeling like some sex-crazed fiend.

As inconspicuously as possible, he reached down and readjusted himself. He'd taken to wearing his shirts untucked for the past week, to save him the embarrassment of everyone seeing that he was in a constant state of semiarousal. Tight jeans had taken a back seat to cargo pants and loose shorts, and for the sake of sperm production, he'd had to trade in his bikini briefs for boxers.

He didn't mind. It was a small sacrifice to make when he considered the end result. When he considered the gift he would be giving Marisa.

And the sex they would be having.

He'd just never anticipated the wait being so…*hard*. It had been well over two weeks and still no ovulation, which translated into no making love. As a result he found himself staring at her constantly when she wasn't looking. Sometimes his imagination would run so far off with his brain, by the time he recovered, she would be staring right back at him with a perplexed look on her face.

The past few days she'd taken to wearing extra layers of clothing, completely obliterating what hint of her figure he'd been able to make out before. He wasn't sure if she was truly embarrassed about her body—which, as far as he could tell, was pretty hot—or just trying to drive him insane.

Or maybe a little of both. Either way, he wouldn't be able to hold out much longer.

"Yo, Jake?"

He realized Tank, the engineer, had been talking to him. "I'm sorry, what did you say?"

Tank nodded toward the booth. "I said Aaron's here."

Jake looked into the booth and sighed. Aaron, their soon-to-be ex-percussionist had finally decided to show up, and, as had been the norm these days, he looked like hell. His clothes were wrinkled and soiled, as if he'd been wearing them for a week. Knowing Aaron, he probably had, and he most likely hadn't showered in a while, either.

Jake slipped from the control room and into the booth. The stench of body odor and liquor hit him like a slap in the face. "Hey, Aaron, nice of you to show up."

"You son of a—"

Jake barely had time to duck before a drumstick flew past his head and crashed into the window behind him. A second stick went airborne and he dodged left.

Well, there was nothing like a concussion to break up the monotony of prolonged abstinence. "I guess you got my message."

"Where's my equipment? And what's this about you getting a new percussionist?"

"Your equipment is packed up and waiting for you in the office. We all talked and decided it would be best if we brought someone else in to finish the CD."

"You can't fire me. I'm the best drummer in this city." Aaron took a threatening step toward him, but Jake didn't flinch. Never let your fear show, that's what Tommy used to tell him. Besides, they had Tank in the next room. All six feet, seven inches and strapping two hundred and twenty pounds of him.

"Aaron, I'm not disputing your abilities. Six months ago you were the best. You still could be. You just need to clean up your act."

"What I need is a job, and a little loyalty from the people I thought were my friends," he spit.

"Loyalty? We've been putting up with this garbage for six months. Half the time you don't show up, and when you do, you play awful. I've repeatedly tried to get you help and you refuse to accept it. You were warned that if you didn't clean up, you would be out. You left me no choice."

Jake saw Louis slip into the booth behind him, shielding his keyboard, ready to intercept Aaron if he went on a total rampage. It wouldn't be the first time. Jake knew from personal experience there was no reasoning with someone in Aaron's condition. More than once Tommy, his own flesh and blood, had turned on him in an alcoholic rage.

"What am I supposed to do now?" Aaron slurred.

"You could start with a couple months of rehab," Jake offered.

"I told you, I don't have a problem." Aaron took another step forward.

Jake held his ground, crossing his arms over his chest. "Don't make things worse than they already are. Just get your stuff and leave. When you're clean, give me a call."

"This isn't over." Aaron finally backed off, tripping over an electrical cord and righting himself against the doorframe, before stumbling into the hall.

"I'm sure it isn't," Jake mumbled. He couldn't help but feel that he'd failed Aaron somehow, that there was something more he could have done to help his friend deal with his addiction. He'd felt the same irrational guilt after Tommy had been arrested that last time.

Jake had tried to take his keys away. He'd warned Tommy not to get behind the wheel, but he hadn't listened.

Louis retrieved the sticks from the floor across the booth. "At least he didn't break anything this time. You think he'll make good on his threat?"

"I don't know. Maybe he'll finally get some help." Jake sighed, shaking his head. "What a way to start the afternoon."

Louis followed him into the control room. "I feel so guilty just tossing him out like that."

"I can't afford to have him wasting our studio time. We're recording this CD on a shoestring as it is. Until he's ready to help himself, there's nothing any of us can do."

Tank looked up as they entered, shrugging sympathetically. "You had no choice, man. He's messed up."

"I know, but it still sucks." Jake collapsed in a chair next to him. His hand strayed up to his shirt pocket, but instead of cigarettes, he found a pack of mints.

The door to the control room swung open and one of the girls from the office stuck her head in. "There's a call for you, Jake."

"Who is it?"

She shrugged. "Some woman."

Jake closed his eyes and let his head fall back. "I'm a little busy here. Can you take a message?"

"I tried, she said it's important. She's on line two."

Cursing, he pulled himself up out of the chair and snatched up the phone, stabbing the button for two. "This better be good."

"Jake?"

"Marisa?" Her voice sounded funny, as if she were inside an echo chamber. "Is that you?"

"We've got two lines."

"Two lines? What are you talking about? Where are you calling me from?"

"I'm in the bathroom, and I have two lines."

"Lines? What lines?"

She laughed. "On the test. One thin and one beautiful big fat purple line."

Lines? Test? His heart clenched in his chest. "Does that mean…?"

"My egg is done cooking."

"Now? As in, right now?"

"As in, how fast can you get here?"

He glanced over at Tank and Louis. Looked like it was going to be an early lunch. "Give me fifteen seconds."

Five

Marisa leaned against the kitchen sink, rechecking the results on the ovulation-kit wand. Yep, it was still positive, though the lines were beginning to fade. That didn't mean she was any less ripe.

According to her cycle, ovulation should have occurred nearly a week ago. Jake—the poor guy—was beginning to show the strain that weeks of celibacy could have on a healthy adult male. To his credit, he hadn't complained, but she could tell he was suffering. More than a few times she'd caught him staring—usually at her breasts—with a hunger in his eyes. A hunger that made her heart race and her knees rubbery.

Not that men didn't look at her that way on a regular basis. It was one of the many unfortunate consequences of having a body like hers. But this was Jake. Her buddy. He never looked at her as anything but a pal. She also realized he was in pretty bad shape if *her* breasts looked appealing to him. Not that they were ugly or deformed. They were just so big. She'd never seen him with a woman who didn't have cute, perky, more-than-a-mouthful-is-a-waste breasts.

Not that her physical appearance mattered. They weren't making love for sexual gratification—at least, she wasn't. They were making a baby. And as badly as she'd wanted a positive test result, to finally get past that first awkward encounter, she was still scared to death.

She was about to have sex—scratch that—*make love* with Jake. *Jake,* her best friend. Unless…

She dropped the wand in the trash and pulled open the drawer next to the stove. From the hall outside her door she heard the thud of footsteps pounding up the stairs. She swallowed hard, then realized she didn't have any saliva left in her mouth. The doorknob turned…

Jake burst through the door of Marisa's apartment, bathed in sweat from having run the three-and-a-half blocks to her building. He shoved the door closed and fell against it. "Boy, am I out of shape."

Marisa stood in the kitchen, eyes wide, a turkey baster clasped in her hand.

Jake propped his hands on his knees, gasping for breath. "Dare I ask what you're planning to do with that? 'Cause I've gotta tell ya', I'm not really into anything that kinky."

"It's nothing, forget it." She tossed it back into the drawer. "Did you run all the way here?"

"The Jeep was blocked in by a delivery truck. I thought it would be faster on foot. Did I miss it?"

"Miss what?"

"Your egg. Is it too late?"

"Oh, I guess I should have explained, my egg is good for at least twenty-four hours after the hormone surge. Sometimes even longer."

"That would have been nice to know." She probably didn't realize it, but, fertile or not, he wasn't leaving this apartment until they'd consummated this arrangement. At least two or three times.

Seventeen years of curiosity would end today.

"I'm really sorry you've had to wait so long." She nervously twirled a lock of hair around her index finger. "I appreciate how patient you've been."

"My patience is running out." He straightened up and took a step toward her—she took one back. He took another step, then another, but for every step he took forward, she retreated. "Marisa, is there something wrong?"

She hooked a thumb over her shoulder. "Maybe we should, um, go in the bedroom."

He shrugged. "The bed, the couch, the floor—wherever you're comfortable. I'm not feeling particularly choosy right now."

Keeping an eye on him, she backed all the way down the hall to her bedroom. The flowery pastels had always been a little too fluffy and feminine for his taste, but now it seemed appropriate. The shades were drawn, giving the room a dim, hazy look and the musky, erotic scent of her perfume drifted in the air.

"I don't like sex."

The statement came out of the clear blue, and he was sure he must have misheard her. "I beg your pardon?"

Marisa stood next to the bed, looking as if she were about to face a firing squad. "I said, I don't like sex. I thought you should know, before we…you know."

"How can you not like sex?"

She shrugged. "I don't know, I just don't. To hear my mother, the way she moaned and groaned and carried on, I thought it would be like heaven on earth. Then I did it and it was just sort of icky."

His brow furrowed. "It was *icky?*"

"I mean, it was painful and embarrassing and messy. I guess I just didn't see the big deal."

"I see," he said. Even though he didn't. Was she trying to say that she hadn't had sex in a while, and maybe she was a little apprehensive? She couldn't mean that she didn't *like* sex. Everybody liked sex, didn't they? "Maybe the men you've been with—"

"Man. There was only one. After a month, when it wasn't getting any better, I came to the conclusion that it just wasn't for me. But that's okay," she hastened to add. "I want it that way. I've never felt I was missing out on anything."

"Wait a minute, when was this? When and with whom did you have this month of offensive sex?"

"Ken Sobleski, my junior year of college."

"You haven't had sex in *six years?*" He tried to keep his jaw from dropping. He knew she didn't date very often. Come to think of it, he couldn't recall the last time she'd been out with a man, but *six years*. Wasn't that unhealthy?

She lay down on the bed and pressed her eyes tightly closed. "Okay, I'm ready. I hope you don't mind, but I'd like to leave most of my clothes on."

When he didn't join her, she opened one eye and saw that he hadn't moved from his spot by the door. He didn't look nearly as intimidating now that he'd lost that I'm-going-to-eat-you-alive expression. When he'd tumbled through her apartment door, sweaty, rumpled and determined, she'd nearly dropped in a dead faint. It had been the precise moment she'd realized he wanted the real thing. He wanted the kind of sex that she'd only read about, maybe wished for a time or two, but didn't have a clue how to deliver.

"The clock is ticking. We should really get started." She closed her eye and tried not to hyperventilate.

There was a long, agonizing silence, then he said, "You seem to be forgetting something."

She opened her eyes and nearly jumped out of her skin. He was standing right over her, gazing down with a hungry grin.

It took all of her concentration to keep her voice from faltering. "What did I forget?"

"We're not going to have sex."

"We're not?"

"We're going to make love. We're getting naked together, Marisa, and no matter what it takes, I'll see to it that we *both* have a good time."

Marisa's heart hammered about a zillion beats per minute. "I appreciate the gesture, Jake, but that's really not necessary."

"It sure as hell is." He reached up and began unfastening his shirt. Though a part of her wanted to look away, her eyes felt glued to his hands as each button popped loose, gradually exposing a narrow band of sun-kissed skin. "Get up. We're going to start doing things my way."

Get up? Where did he intend to take her?

Was he going to make her do it somewhere exotic, like the kitchen table? She wasn't sure if she was ready for anything that adventurous—if she would *ever* be ready for it.

She sat up, surprised to feel herself trembling. Why would she be afraid? This was Jake, her best friend. A man she trusted implicitly. "You don't want to do it here?"

"Eventually, yes. First, I need a shower." He unfastened the last button, but didn't remove his shirt. "While I do that, I want you to go in the kitchen and pour yourself a glass of wine, put some soft music on and try to relax a little."

It wasn't supposed to be like this. She had figured they would just hop into bed and get it over with. When he'd come in earlier he certainly looked ready. Why was he stalling now?

Because he wanted to…satisfy her. Well, some people weren't built that way. She just happened to be *some* people.

She followed him to the bathroom. "Did I do something wrong?"

He stopped in the doorway and turned to her. Again her eyes were drawn to the front of his shirt. Why had seeing his chest suddenly become such a source of fascination? It wasn't as though she'd never seen it before. And why did he look so tall today? Had he always been this tall?

And his eyes—were they always this shocking blue? Had they always fixed on her so intently, as if he could see past all of her defenses and into her soul?

"You haven't done a thing wrong," he said. "I just never anticipated how uneasy you would be. If we weren't on a schedule so to speak, I would stop this right here and work into the whole thing a little bit slower. I almost feel I'm doing this against your will."

Her breath caught. That was the last thing she wanted him to feel. She wanted this. More than she'd ever wanted anything in her life. So much it scared her. "*No*. Jake, you're not—"

"I know I'm not. But we need to take this a little bit slower. Here I was, ready to jump into bed with you at a moment's notice and I've never even kissed you. Doesn't that seem a little backward?"

He definitely had a point. Maybe if they took things slower she wouldn't feel so inept. "I guess maybe it does."

He took a step toward her. "Can I kiss you now?"

It was funny, but in every possible scenario she'd imagined, a thing as basic as kissing had never crossed her mind. His mouth touching her mouth, his lips against her lips, his tongue—

A ripple of sensation zinged through her when she imagined that. Not that she hadn't kissed him before. There was that one time. But kissing didn't really count when half the party was unconscious, did it? It would be decidedly more fun with him participating.

"Yes," she said, surprised by how breathy and deep her voice sounded. "I want you to kiss me."

He stepped closer, until they were almost touching. She could feel a wave of heat radiating from his body, smell the vague, intoxicating scent of sweat intermingled with his cologne. Breathing seemed to take extra effort as she lost herself in the ocean-blue of his eyes.

His hand came up, stilled just shy of her face, then he tentatively cupped her cheek. His fingers were long and graceful, his touch gentle. *The hands of a musician,* she thought. Hands that she wanted on her body.

The intensity of that sudden desire made her breath hitch.

Jake's hand fell to his side and he stepped away.

"I'm sorry!" This time she made a move toward him. "You don't have to—"

"Yes, I do." His voice cracked on the last word. He

drew back, into the bathroom. "Just give me five minutes."

"But—"

"I *need* five minutes," he said, closing the door.

Jake tore off his sweaty clothes and blasted the shower on cold. Steeling himself, he stepped under the icy spray. Touching her cheek, seeing the sudden flash of heat in her eyes, the flush of her skin—it had almost set him off.

Groaning, he pressed his forehead against the cold tile as icy water sluiced down his shoulders and back. He couldn't remember a time in his life when he'd felt more turned on by the idea of making love to a woman. When the mere thought of kissing her had nearly set him off. Maybe it was the waiting, the anticipation of making love, or their deep respect and friendship—a bond that had persevered more than half his life. Or was it that element of naughtiness, the idea of tasting the forbidden fruit. And he did want to taste her.

No, no, no, don't think about that.

He grabbed a bar of soap, lathered his arms and chest. The throb in his groin had him wishing he could slide his hand down and give himself some relief. She would never know, and the worst that would happen is it would take an extra month to conceive. Big hardship. But this wasn't about him, about his satisfaction. This was about Marisa, and her baby. He would never go back on his word. If that meant climaxing on the first thrust like some inexperienced teenager and mangling his pride, well then, he'd just have to live with that. And hope she didn't laugh too hard.

Now, if he could just make it to the first thrust.

After lathering and rinsing the rest of his body, he

stepped out of the shower. He quickly toweled off, pulled his pants back on, then headed to the kitchen. The stereo was off, the wine bottle on the counter untouched and Marisa was nowhere to be seen. "Marisa?"

"Back here," she called. "In the bedroom."

Jake appeared in the bedroom doorway, cargo pants slung low on his hips, chest bare and still glistening with beads of moisture. His stomach was smooth and defined, bisected by a band of downy hair that vanished under his waistband. His hair was mussed, as if he'd hastily rubbed it dry with a towel and hadn't wasted any time with a comb. It made him look disheveled and sexy and…desirable.

When he spotted her on the bed, covered to her chin under the blanket, he clutched the doorframe and cursed softly. Through the dusty light of the lavender-scented candles she'd lit, she saw him suck in a deep breath.

"You're in bed," he said.

She nodded to the pile of clothes on the chair across the room. "And I'm naked."

"Completely naked?"

"Why don't you come find out for yourself."

When Jake had pulled away from her in the hallway—or more specifically, when she'd figured out *why* he pulled away—everything had shifted. Her fear melted away.

This man, her best friend in the world, had spent agonizing weeks of celibacy simply because she'd asked him to. It only seemed fair to make this satisfying for him. She wanted more than anything to give him at least that. Maybe it would be good for her, too. And if it wasn't, that would be all right. Knowing she was pleasing him would be satisfying enough.

He walked to the bed, unfastening his pants. "Are you *sure* you're ready for this?"

She looked down at his zipper. "I don't know. Is there something in there that's going to scare me?"

He laughed lightly. "I meant, are you ready for this?" He nodded toward the bed. "Maybe we should start in the living room and work our way back here. Take our time."

"I don't know about you, but I think we've waited long enough. And I think you need to lose the clothes, now."

"You're the boss." His pants dropped to the carpet and—oh boy, Ken Sobleski hadn't looked *anything* like that. Jake's body was long and lean and muscular. And beautiful. God, he was beautiful. It amazed her that he could be so completely nonchalant about his nudity— so comfortable in his own skin. And she couldn't seem to get her fill of looking at him.

He climbed into bed, mindful not to disturb the blankets covering her. Propping himself up on one elbow, he gazed down at her, a ridiculously sexy smile on his face.

She waited for him to make the first move—to kiss her, to touch her. To do *something*. He only grinned.

"What?" she asked.

"You look cute all covered up, but—" he tugged lightly on the covers "—how about showing me some skin."

Okay, here we go. She closed her eyes, took a deep breath and held it as he slowly nudged the covers down, until the tops of her shoulders were exposed. The air felt cool against her skin.

"Breathe, Marisa, you're turning blue."

She let the breath out in a gusty rush. "Sorry. I'm just a little apprehensive. Not too many people have seen me naked."

He eased the blanket lower, revealing the very tops of her breasts. "Why is that?"

"My body, it's just so…"

With the lightest touch, he traced the curve of her breast just above the edge of the blanket, and she completely lost her train of thought. "Just so what?"

"Suffice it to say, I have issues."

Reaching down, he took her hand from under the covers and pressed her palm to the center of his chest. "Can you feel that? Would my heart beat like this if your body didn't turn me on?"

His heart lunged in his chest, much like her own. His skin was smooth and hot to the touch, the muscles firm underneath. She could barely believe this was Jake lying beside her. Jake touching her this way.

"Marisa," he said, his voice husky. "Can I kiss you?"

Fearing her voice would betray her, she closed her eyes and tilted her chin up in a silent invitation. The whisper of his breath, warm and scented with mint, tantalized her. Then his mouth brushed against her own and everything inside of her went limp. His lips were soft and gentle, his mouth hot and sweet. The fragrance of her soap, united with his own masculine, enticing scent, made her dizzy.

Kissing Jake came so naturally, was such a perfect fit, it was as if they'd been kissing each other this way their whole lives.

When he pulled away, Marisa opened her eyes. Her lids felt heavy, her body boneless.

Jake smiled down at her. "That was nice."

"Yes, it was."

"Ready for more?"

Was she ever. She wrapped her hands around the back of his neck and pulled him down. He groaned and leaned into her, his skin hot against hers. This time the kiss was deeper, more urgent. And when his hand came up to gently cradle her face, when his fingers tangled in her hair, an ember smoldering low in her belly sparked and flames licked at her insides, setting her on fire. Ken Sobleski had definitely never made her feel this way. He'd been rough and clumsy and never gave a thought to making her feel good.

She hadn't imagined it was possible to feel like this.

Her body responded to his kiss, taking on a will of its own. Her hands moved up his chest, tentatively exploring the taut muscle underneath. His shoulders felt broad and powerful, his skin smooth and damp from his shower.

She felt drunk on desire, intoxicated by the flavor of his mouth, lulled by the slow, sensual rhythm of his tongue. She tunneled her fingers through his wet hair, sank her nails into his shoulders, urging him closer.

A low moan exploded from his throat and he tore his mouth from hers. He manacled her wrists and pinned them above her head. "Slow down," he warned.

The way he held her captive was as exciting as it was frustrating. Now that she'd started, had a small taste of what was to come, she didn't want to slow down.

With his free hand he tugged the covers away and she was too deeply under his spell to care that she was completely exposed—naked to him in body and mind. Then he gently cupped one breast, dipping his head to taste her.

"*Oh—*" Her body pressed up toward his mouth.

"You like that?" he murmured.

Like? Like couldn't adequately describe what she was feeling. There wasn't a single word in the entire English language that could describe what he was doing to her. And still she wanted more. She wanted to touch him, to be touched. She *ached* for it.

His hand came to rest on her stomach and peaks of heat exploded under the surface of her skin, leaving a trail of fire as he wandered lower. She instinctively arched up in anticipation.

Jake lifted his head and a smile curled his lips. "At the risk of sounding smug, yours are definitely not the reactions of a woman who doesn't like sex."

"Maybe I'm faking it," she said, her voice little more than a breathy gasp.

"Well then," he said with a wicked grin, "I'll just have to try harder."

Six

Jake drew one nipple deep into the heat of his mouth, never taking his eyes off her face and Marisa's body rocked up, arms pressed against his restraining hand. His other hand wandered lower still, parting her, until all the blood in her body seemed to shoot down, swirling and pulsing where he stroked, leaving her dizzy and breathless. Hot and cold all at the same time. He played her body like a finely tuned instrument, striking cords deep inside, reaching a fever pitch. Until it was too much, *too* intense.

"Oh, Jake," she gasped. She struggled to free her arms but had neither the strength nor the will to give it a valiant effort.

"Let it out, Marisa, let it happen."

She shook her head. "I can't. It's too much."

But don't ever stop, she wanted to beg. *Never stop touching me.*

"Yes, you can." He released her hands and sank down in the bed, parting her thighs with the width of his shoulders. Her first instinct was to pull her legs together, to push him away. The stubble on his chin chafed her as he pressed a kiss to the sensitive flesh on her inner thigh and she sucked in a surprised breath. She planted a restraining hand on the top of his head. "Jake, don't—"

"Let me, Marisa," he said. "Let me taste you."

He lowered his head and the first sweep of his tongue, the sheer intimacy of his actions, tore her apart. Instead of pushing him away, she hooked her fingers through his hair, holding him in place.

Pleasure surged in a hot rush, carried her higher and higher, until she felt as if she were floating above the bed. Pure sensation, excruciating in its intensity, assaulted her from every direction at once. And just when she thought it couldn't get any better, when she thought she'd reached irrevocable bliss, he concentrated his movements on one tiny sensitive spot and—

"Oh, *Jake!*" Every cell in her body overflowed, screaming in ecstasy. All of her senses melted together, fused. Muscles clenched and locked. Her mind soared, suspending her high, high above herself. It seemed to go on forever, until she thought she really would die from the painful perfection of it all, then very slowly, very gently she spiraled back down. Sated and limp, she curled her arms around Jake. She opened her eyes to see him smiling at her, his skin flushed, lids half-closed.

"And I thought *I* had pent up sexual tension," he said, brushing back the hair that had fallen over her face. "I thought you were going to burst into flames."

"That was…wow. You hear women talk about it,

and you read about it in books, but when you actually feel it, it's just…''

"Wow?"

"Yeah. *Wow.*"

Jake's grin widened with male pride and Marisa reached up, touched his face. She traced the lines around his mouth, smoothed the tiny creases in the corners of his eyes, amazed that she was really touching him this way, that she couldn't *not* touch him. It felt natural. Right. His skin was warm and damp and bronzed from the sun, the stubble on his chin rough against her palm. She could see his pulse throbbing through the arteries in his neck.

Locking her hands behind his head, she pulled him down for a kiss. His mouth was hot and tangy, tender yet demanding.

"Make love to me, Jake," she murmured, sliding her hands down his back, over his smooth, muscular backside. The muscles clenched under her palms.

"Go slow," he groaned as she pulled him into the cradle of her thighs. "I don't want to hurt you."

"You won't hurt me." She felt an almost desperate need to complete what they had started. To make that connection. She *ached* for it somewhere deep inside herself. An empty place that nothing, not even Jake's friendship, had ever been able to fill.

Twining her legs through his, she boldly arched against him. Jake let out a gasping breath, tightening his arms around her. He pushed forward slowly, concentration sharpening the planes of his face. And there was no pain, only exquisite perfection. Their bodies fit just right, as though they had been built for each other.

This was nothing like it had been with, with… whatever his name was. This was sweet, tender. No one but Jake could touch her this way. No one but Jake could make her *feel* this way.

He plunged deep and steady, eyes closed, head thrown back. The corded muscles in his neck and shoulders tensed into tight bands. He was holding back, when all she wanted him to do was let go.

"Jake, open your eyes."

"I can't," he groaned, sinking deeper still, touching a place that had never been touched before. A place so deep, it felt as if he'd reached her soul.

He was so close she could feel it. She needed to know that it was her face he saw when it happened. She had to know if this was real. "Please, look at me."

His eyes opened, dark and turbulent like crashing waves in a storm. The second they fixed on her, his control splintered. His body coiled and spasmed. Marisa held him tight, cradling him through his release.

With a throaty groan he settled into her, resting his head on her shoulder, fighting to catch his breath. "I'm sorry."

She sighed, stroking his damp hair. "I can't imagine why."

"You didn't come. I wanted to hold out."

"Jake, get real. Another orgasm like the first one would have knocked me unconscious. It couldn't have been more perfect."

He realized that he was probably crushing her, but when he tried to roll away, tried to break their bond, she locked her legs through his, holding him prisoner.

"Not yet," she whispered.

He nuzzled his face into the silken skin of her neck. Knowing how long it had been for her, he had hoped to take it slow and easy. To make it last. He wanted it to be special. But she was so damned tight, so hot. "Did I hurt you?"

"It was perfect." She idly traced the line of his jaw with her thumb. "Do you think it worked. Do you think I'm pregnant?"

"I—I don't know." He'd almost forgotten why they were lying there together. And then it hit him. This wasn't real. She wasn't clinging to him out of sentimentality or affection. She just didn't want any of his precious genetic material lost.

The realization left him feeling cold and empty. He found himself hoping it hadn't worked, hoping it took months and months, until he was ready for this to end— and instantly felt a sweep of guilt for his selfishness.

This wasn't about him. This was about Marisa, about the baby. That was the only thing he should be thinking about. He wanted this for her, for himself even in a way.

But never in his life had a fantasy paled in comparison to the real thing. Sex to him had always been about satisfaction, about achieving a goal. His emotions rarely played a role, and love certainly never factored into the equation. Love and respect were what had driven him today.

Making love to Marisa was like nothing he'd ever experienced. And, he feared, like nothing he ever would again.

He could only hope that in a few months they would have had their fill of each other, then they could go back to the way things had been before. Maybe it would be enough by then. He could return to the shallow existence, where emotionally he kept everyone at arm's length. Everyone except Marisa.

And what if a few months together wasn't enough? What if it was *never* enough?

Marisa glanced over at the clock on her bedside table. "Shoot, I told Lucy she could leave early today. I have to get downstairs."

Whether it was the truth or just an excuse to get them out of what could quickly become an awkward position, it didn't matter. He couldn't let these warm fuzzy feelings he was having get the better of him. "I told everyone at the studio to take a long lunch. I'm sure they're back by now."

He rolled away from her and reached for his clothes. They would both be better off if they pretended everything was normal. As if they met for a quick roll in the hay all the time. No big deal.

"So, you uh, want to get together tonight?" he asked, sitting on the edge of the bed, his back to her. "I mean, should we give it another try, in case it didn't work this time? You'll still be fertile, right?"

"I should be. But Lucy and I are supposed to do inventory tonight. I'd cancel, but we're already behind in getting the fall stock out. How about an early lunch tomorrow?"

In other words, she'd had enough for one day. That was okay. This was an adjustment for them both. "Tomorrow is good."

A loud rap on the apartment door startled them both. Like two guilty teenagers caught in a compromising position by their parents, they sprang out of the bed and dived for their clothes.

"Who is that?" Jake whispered, even though there was no way the person knocking could hear them.

"I don't know, maybe it's Lucy coming to get me." She grabbed her dress and yanked it over her head. "How are we going to explain this?"

Whoever was at the door rapped impatiently.

"We don't have to explain a thing. Just answer the door and act as if nothing is going on." He hastily pulled his pants on, but his shirt and boxers were still in the bathroom. "I'm going to clean up and get dressed. Just act normal."

While Jake locked himself in the bathroom, Marisa ran to the door, combing her fingers through her hair. The pounding became louder, more urgent, and when she swung the door open, Julia, her father's fiancée, fell through.

"There's a madman after me with a cheese grater," Julia squealed, cowering behind her. Marisa looked out in the hallway, just in time to see Mr. Kloppman's door close.

"Don't worry, he's harmless. He's a little senile, but he wouldn't hurt a flea." She closed the door and Julia heaved a sigh of relief.

"Thank goodness!" She stood in the middle of the living room, visibly shaken, clutching her purse to her chest. In skintight flared jeans and a silk short-sleeved blouse, she looked even younger than she had that night in the store. "He called me an alien."

"Yeah, well, he's kind of an *X-Files* fanatic." Aware that she hadn't put on a bra, Marisa casually crossed her arms over her breasts. "Um, what are you doing here?"

"I wanted to give you this." Julia held out an envelope. "I wanted to hand-deliver the invitation, and tell you again how much it means to us that you're coming."

Marisa took the invitation. "You could have saved yourself the trip and mailed it to me."

Julia inched toward the door, brow furrowed. "I'm sorry, I've come at a bad time."

"N-no, of course not. I was getting ready for work. I just meant that you didn't have to waste your time coming here. You probably have wedding plans to worry about or something."

"I tried the store first, but Lucy said you were here. She thought it would be okay if I came up. I hope I haven't interrupted anything."

From behind her, Marisa heard the toilet flush, then the squeak of the bathroom door opening. Jake appeared a second later, his shirt wrinkled, his hair damp and disheveled.

Could his timing have been any worse?

"Jake, you remember Julia," Marisa said.

Julia looked at Jake, then Marisa, and did a pretty horrible job of trying not to smirk. "It's nice to see you again, Jake."

Jake gave Julia a vague smile. "Uh, Marisa, I really have to get to the studio, I'll talk to you tomorrow."

Marisa opened the door for him. "See you later," she called. He didn't spare her a second glance as he disappeared down the stairs. She knew the plan had been to act as if nothing was out of the ordinary, but after the things he'd done to her...

She sighed quietly, then turned back to Julia. "If there was nothing else you needed, I really have to get downstairs."

"I just wanted to give you the invitation and make sure you still planned on attending."

"I said I would."

"I wanted to be sure. I got the distinct impression you and your father don't get along."

Young *and* smart. They were batting two for two. "I promise, I'll be there."

"I won't keep you any longer." She started out the

door but paused in the hall. "By the way, you might want to dab a little powder on your cheeks to cover the flush. And before you go down, be sure to turn your dress right side in."

Busted. Marisa opened her mouth to speak but couldn't think of a single thing to say.

"Don't worry, your secret is safe with me," Julia said, and her smile was so genuine, so eager, Marisa believed her.

She also couldn't help wondering what she and Jake had just gotten themselves into.

Marisa glanced at her watch for the thousandth time that morning then gazed with frustration at the customers browsing the store. Not that she wasn't thrilled to have the business, especially after several stagnant weeks, but if it didn't slow down soon, she wouldn't have time for lunch with Jake. She'd promised to call him when she was able to sneak away, but it was already eleven-thirty. Technically she wouldn't be fertile for much longer, possibly rendering their impending encounter completely unnecessary.

"Your total is sixty-eight o-four," she told the customer on the opposite side of the counter and hurriedly completed the transaction.

Although she would never admit it to Jake, she couldn't imagine waiting an entire month to make love again. Or never making love to him again if the first time had worked and she was already pregnant. When she was growing up, the idea of sex was something ugly and rough. It was the sharp thud of her mother's headboard smashing into the bedroom wall. The animal-like groans of her frequent and varied partners. Marisa's college experiences had only compounded her misconception.

With Jake, it was beautiful. It was about connecting, about creating a life. And of course there was the physical pleasure. He'd awakened a desire in her she hadn't dreamed existed. The mere thought of him in her bed, feeling his hands on her body again, touching him in return, sent her already overactive hormones into a rage.

"Adding the oils and candles was a fantastic idea," Lucy said, joining her behind the counter. Marisa moved aside so Lucy could ring up her customer.

She bagged the customer's purchases then turned to Marisa. "Are you okay? Your cheeks are flushed."

The fact that Marisa had been so caught up in her fantasies only intensified the blush in her cheeks. This wasn't like her, not at all. She really should be ashamed of herself. But for some reason she wasn't. She felt alive—feminine and desirable and beautiful.

Lucy pressed cool fingers to Marisa's face. "Jeez, you're burning up. Are you sick?"

"I do feel a little woozy." It wasn't a complete lie. She did feel woozy, just not for the reason Lucy assumed.

"Why don't you take the rest of the afternoon off? Take a nap or something."

"I suppose a little time in bed wouldn't hurt." That was the God's honest truth. She needn't mention she wouldn't be there alone. "I'm going to head up. You sure you'll be okay?"

"Take all the time you need."

"Thanks, Luce. Call if you need me."

Marisa headed up the back stairs, making a quick scan-stop at Mr. Kloppman's door on her way into her apartment. Once inside, she grabbed the cordless phone off the kitchen counter. She hit speed dial and waited for someone to answer at the studio, then waited another five minutes while they found Jake.

"Hey," she said, when he answered. "It's me."

"What's up?" he said gruffly.

Disappointment curled through her stomach. Could he be mad at her? Had she done something wrong? "Is everything okay?"

His voice softened. "Yeah, sorry. Bad morning, money issues. I didn't mean to snap at you."

"Do you want me to call you back later?"

"No, now is good. I could use a break."

"Oh, well, why don't you come over."

There was a brief silence, then he said, "Come over?"

"Yeah, to my place." He had to know what she meant. Had he forgotten already?

"For...?" he asked.

"For *sex,* Jake. I'm inviting you over to make love." She heard what sounded like a sigh of relief.

"Just checking. I didn't want to overstep my bounds."

"You'll have to sneak up the street entrance without Lucy seeing you."

"I'm already gone," he said, and she heard the phone clatter as he hastily hung up.

That was more like it. For a second there, she'd begun to think he'd had a change of heart.

To kill time until he arrived, Marisa brushed her teeth, fixed her hair and applied fresh mascara. She adjusted the blinds in the bedroom, then lit the candles on her bedside table. On a whim, she slid the top drawer of the bureau open, extracting the package she'd hidden there weeks before, when Jake had agreed to this. She'd chosen it with him in mind, unsure if she'd ever have the courage to wear it.

Separating the folds of pink tissue, she lifted the gown from the wrapping. She stripped out of her clothes and tugged it over her head. The slippery black fabric hugged her body, molding to every conceivable crease and curve, plunging low in the front and barely containing her breasts. What wasn't hanging out was scantily covered by transparent lace.

It looked so ridiculous, so blatantly sexual, she shook her head in disgust. What had she been thinking? She looked like the cover of some sleazy men's magazine. She normally wouldn't be caught dead in anything this clingy and revealing. And she knew without a doubt she couldn't let Jake see her this way. Not in a million years.

"How did you know?"

Marisa gasped and spun around, backing into the bureau so hard the collection of bottles and vials it held toppled over and rolled off. Jake stood watching her, leaning casually against the doorframe, arms folded over his chest.

Marisa's hand flew up in a hopeless effort to cover herself. *Shoot, shoot, shoot!* How did he get there so fast? "I didn't hear you come in."

Jake circled the bed, peeling his T-shirt over his head and tossing it to the floor. She stood frozen, following his eyes as they trailed hungrily down her body. Well, that was definitely the reaction she'd hoped for, so why did she feel so uneasy? So phony?

"How did you know I like black," he asked, stopping in front of her.

"Black?"

"The gown." He brushed his fingers across the silky

fabric clinging like a second skin to her hip. "It's, *wow.*"

"What, this old thing?" She tried to sound casual, but her voice was far too wobbly to be convincing. She just wasn't cut out for this seduction stuff. It wasn't in her nature.

His hand curved over her hip, slid slowly up. "Did you pick this out for me?"

He slipped a finger beneath one of the thin straps holding up the gown. Barely grazing her skin with the tip of his finger, he caressed up to her shoulder and down again to the crest of her breast.

A rush of erotic sensation made her knees wobbly and her blood pump faster. She felt torn between the need to touch him, to be touched, and the deep embarrassment of being caught this way.

"Tell the truth, Marisa. Is this for me?"

"Yes," she admitted, not surprised that he'd seen through her feeble attempt to seduce him, to try to mold herself into the kind of woman he desired. But this wasn't her. "I thought it might…help."

"I've been fantasizing about you wearing black lingerie for weeks," he said.

Fantasizing? About her? For *weeks?* For a second she was too dumbfounded to reply. "H-how many weeks?"

His brow furrowed. "Too many."

She was about to ask him how many was too many, but the gentle scrape of his teeth on her shoulder, the whisper of his breath on her skin, temporarily scattered any coherent thought. Still she couldn't escape the nagging feeling that this was all wrong. That she wasn't being honest with him.

She pulled out of his arms and backed away. "I'm sorry. I tried, but I can't do this."

Seven

Jake looked perplexed. "What's wrong?"

"What's *wrong?* Look at me." She threw out her arms. "I look ridiculous. I wear men's T-shirts and flannel pajamas to bed. This isn't me."

"So, why did you wear it?"

"You said it yourself—you like black lingerie."

He shrugged. "So what?"

She lowered her eyes, too ashamed to look at him. "I was just trying to make it *fun* for you. I wanted it to be special."

"What made you think it wouldn't be special?"

"I'm not blind. I see the kind of women you're attracted to. That's just not me."

"Marisa, look in the mirror."

She shook her head. "I don't want to."

When she didn't move, Jake took her by the shoulders, gently turning her to face the mirror. He stood behind her, his hands on her shoulders. "Don't you know, my attraction to you has nothing to do with lingerie. It isn't about the kind of clothes you wear, or even what your body looks like. It's about what's inside." He pressed a hand over her heart. "What's in here. That's what attracts me to you."

There was a sincerity in his eyes, a deep respect that nearly brought her to tears. He slid his other hand across her stomach, eased her to him.

"Thank you." She leaned into him, rubbing her cheek against his solid chest. His heart thumped in her ear.

He tucked her hair out of the way and pressed a lingering kiss to her throat. "Are you in any hurry to get back downstairs, or can Lucy handle things without you?"

"She told me to take my time."

"Good, because I gave the guys the rest of the afternoon off. Now let's get you out of this thing." He gathered the gown in his fists and she raised her arms so he could peel it up over her head. Her hair cascaded down, falling over her shoulders in soft waves, resting on the tops of her breasts. "Better?"

She nodded, gasping lightly as he reached around and flattened both hands over her stomach, sliding one slowly upward. He watched over her shoulder, following his actions in the mirror. Watching him watch her with heavy-lidded eyes, seeing his hand slide up, cup the weight of her breast in his palm, tease her nipple between his fingers, made her skin come alive with sensation. She moaned and closed her eyes, letting her head fall back to rest against his chest.

"You're so beautiful, Marisa," he murmured against

her neck, his mouth hot on her skin. "I love touching you. Making you feel good."

He slipped the other hand lower, between her thighs. When his fingers brushed across the sensitive flesh there, her body quaked. He stroked once, twice, a third time, and she clamped her teeth down on her lip to prevent herself from crying out.

Fearing her legs would give out, she wrapped her arms around his neck, leaning in to him. The friction was painfully intense, torturous even, and she never wanted it to end. But she could feel the pressure building, feel herself slipping under.

"Marisa," Jake said, his voice low and husky. "Look in the mirror. Look at us."

She opened her eyes, saw the two of them bound tightly together, skin to skin, soul to soul, and she shattered. A cry of pleasure ripped from her throat and her knees buckled from under her.

Jake held her close through her release, never taking his eyes off her reflection, hypnotized as pleasure pulsed through her body. It was the most erotic thing he'd ever seen. It astounded him that she would think a scrap a black silk could heighten his desire. His attraction to her, his need, was absolute. Nothing she wore, or didn't wear, could make him want her more.

Yet, never in his wildest dreams had he expected it to be this…*good*. Never had he connected to another human being so completely. In body and mind and spirit.

It scared him half out of his mind.

Every instinct he possessed told him he wasn't good enough for her. And as badly as he wanted to be, he would never be a good enough father to the child they were trying to create. He also knew, with absolute certainty, Marisa was strong enough, mature enough to take on the responsibility alone. The baby would be lucky to have her.

Marisa turned in his arms, rising up on her toes to kiss him. The second his lips parted, she thrust her tongue inside. Her lips were soft, her mouth sweet and full of promise.

He felt a tug as she unfastened the button on his pants, heard the hiss of his zipper as she lowered it. It filled him with an almost giddy anticipation. Every touch, every taste, every breath they shared, was an adventure into the unknown.

Without breaking their kiss, she impatiently shoved his pants down his legs and he kicked them out of the way. She grasped the waist of his boxers, her fingers brushing against his bare stomach, making the muscles coil. He fisted his hands through her hair, felt himself spinning out of control. He never let himself lose control, never surrendered everything to a woman. Now he couldn't seem to hold anything back.

Marisa tugged Jake's boxers down, awed by the sight of all that male perfection. She'd never really considered the male anatomy anything but mysterious and maybe a little threatening, but Jake—he was beautiful beyond words. She reached down, circled his shaft in her hand, stroked him, feeling all the different textures, marveling at the contrast of soft, smooth skin over solid heat.

Jake muffled a moan into her neck. His eyes were closed, his face flushed. "That feels so good, Marisa. But I don't know how much more I can take."

She wanted so badly to keep going. She had to remind herself once again that they weren't doing this for the fun of it—at least, not completely. They were trying to conceive. That should have been the only thing on her mind. She almost felt guilty.

Almost.

Would it really be so bad to take a little bit for herself? To enjoy this?

Jake lay back on the bed, pulling Marisa on top of him. He slid his hands up her back and shoulders, easing her down for a deep, soul-searching kiss. His tongue seemed to fill her as he lazily explored her mouth. She found herself unconsciously moving her hips, pressing herself against him.

"Make love to *me* this time," he said. "Just like this."

She hesitated. "I—I don't know what to do."

"Do whatever feels good."

She centered herself over him and sank down slowly, reveling in the absolute perfection of taking him inside of her body, of making that connection. She rocked her hips in a slow, steady rhythm. The sensation was exquisite—torturously wonderful—yet she wasn't quite…

"Marisa," Jake whispered, as if he could barely expend the energy to speak. His eyes were closed in concentration and sweat beaded his forehead. "I'm getting really close."

"Go ahead," she said, leaning forward to press her lips to his.

He held her back. "No, not without you."

"I—I don't think I can."

"Yes, *you can.* Sit up. Sit up then try leaning back. Rest your hands on my thighs."

It was awkward for a second, until she established her balance, but she didn't see how this would—

He thrust his hips up hard and fast and the sensation rocked through her like a bolt of white lightning.

"*Oh!*" She clutched his thighs, digging her nails into his skin. "What did you do?"

He thrust again and she nearly screamed from the intense stab of pleasure.

"Oh, do it again."

Jake thrust again, then again. He'd always prided himself on his ability to please a woman, but he wasn't sure if he'd ever pleased one quite like this. For every thrust, she cried out, and every lustful cry pushed him closer to the edge, but after his pitiful performance yesterday, he refused to let himself come first.

When he couldn't stand it any longer, he flipped her onto her back. Her legs instantly locked around his waist and her back arched. He drove into her hard and swift, half-afraid he was going to hurt her. But she urged him on with thick moans, dragging her nails across his back, digging her fingers through his hair. Almost instantly he felt the muscles surrounding him clench in a fistlike grip as she reached her climax. He locked midthrust and he came so hard he swore his body would turn itself inside out from the momentum.

When he came back down to earth, she lay beneath him, soft and warm and breathing hard. For the longest time neither uttered a word.

"Jake," Marisa finally whispered.

He leaned down, kissed her cheeks and eyelids, the tip of her nose. "Hmm?"

"Is making love always like that?"

He almost laughed at the absurdity of her question. This was as much a mystery to him as it was to her. "I don't think it's ever been quite like that."

He kissed her, felt her lips curve into a smile.

"I think I changed my mind," she murmured.

"'Bout what?"

"I *really* like sex. I like it so much, I think we should make love again."

"You up for a shopping trip this weekend?"

Lucy looked up from rack of silk thongs she'd been sorting by color and size. "Have I ever passed up an excuse to shop? What's the occasion?"

"My father's wedding." Marisa propped her elbows on the counter and dropped her chin on the backs of her hands. "I need a new dress. I was thinking of something in black, maybe above the knee."

"What's up with that?" Lucy asked, shoving a hand through her unruly curls.

Marisa shrugged. "With what?"

"Look at you. Your skirt doesn't hang down to your ankles and that blouse actually shows some cleavage. Did you lose weight or something?"

"I don't think so."

"Don't misunderstand me, I think you look great."

Marisa looked down at herself, feeling a little tug of pride. She did look pretty good. Lately, the full, drapy clothing just made her feel...frumpy. The attention she drew from strange men had always made her feel cheap. Like her mother, who epitomized the word *cheap*. Since she and Jake had started the baby campaign, however, she'd begun to feel differently about her body: desirable, and powerful in a way she'd never appreciated before. Maybe the change was simply due to the fact that she was finally accepting herself and realizing that, just because she looked like her mother, she wasn't destined to be like her.

"Well, whatever the reason," Lucy said. "I think it's great. Now all we have to do is find you a man."

Already got one, thanks. For a few days a month anyway, Marisa reminded herself. Unfortunately the first attempt had been a failure. She'd started her period only three days after they'd made love. She'd never been particularly regular, the slightest change in environment throwing her cycle off by days, sometimes weeks. More than likely, she'd been so nervous about their venture into the unknown, her systen had gone haywire.

Jake had been so sweet and understanding when she'd told him it hadn't worked. He'd held her while she sniffled back tears of disappointment then tucked her into bed with a heating pad and a cup of herbal tea. He'd had so much studio work lately, time for his own music had been limited, but he'd stayed with her through the worst of it. When even the painkillers her doctor had prescribed didn't ease the intense pain.

Although, truth be told, it hadn't been as bad this month. Sure, she'd been in a lot of pain, but not the incapacitating pain that sometimes kept her off her feet for several days. She'd spent one day in bed, and by the following morning she was back to work.

And in a few weeks they would try again, she thought without the barest trace of apprehension. This time she was looking forward to it, craving it even.

As desperately as she wanted a baby, after she got over the grief of their failure, she couldn't stop herself from feeling a little bit relieved. It's not that she wasn't ready to be a mother. She'd been preparing herself financially and emotionally for several years, waiting for the right time. With a considerable nest egg in the bank and the flexibility of being her own boss and making her own hours, she could now give the baby everything it needed.

What she hadn't anticipated was the way she felt

about Jake. Maybe it was selfish, but she wanted to spend a little more time with him as lovers.

"I've noticed Jake watching you a lot lately," Lucy said in a singsong voice.

Marisa looked over at her, forced a laugh. "He has not."

Had he? No, he wouldn't. They had both been very careful about keeping their friendship and the baby-making process quite separate. Since the last time they made love, he'd made no mention of sex, and he certainly hadn't acted as if he desired her. On the contrary, they both seemed to be avoiding absolutely any physical contact.

And quite frankly it was frustrating the heck out of her. He made it look so easy, when deep down, it was driving her mad.

"He has so. When your back is turned I see him watching your every move." Lucy draped a thong from her index finger, grinning wickedly. "I think Jake has a secret crush on you."

"Trust me, he doesn't."

Lucy stretched the thong between her fingers and shot it at Marisa like a rubber band. "I also think that deep down, you love him."

She caught the thong and tossed it back. "I do love him."

"I mean that you're *in* love with him," Lucy said, and when Marisa opened her mouth to speak, she waved a hand at her. "I know, neither of you ever wants to get married, blah, blah, blah. I've heard it all before, and I think you're both emotionally retarded. What's the point in life if you can't share it with someone special, someone you love. Who better than your best friend?"

"We just don't have that kind of relationship." Well, not usually. "Even if we did find each other appealing…" Major understatement there. "…there's the slight problem of me wanting a child and him having no interest in kids." Huge problem. "Either way you look at it, it would never work."

The bells above the door jingled and when Marisa looked over, she did her best to mask her sudden wariness. "Hello, Julia."

"Hi, Marisa, Lucy." Julia stepped tentatively inside. She wore a pair of flat sandals and a simple summer dress. She was really quite small without the monster heels, which of course made her look even younger. Marisa placed her at about sixteen today.

"The store looks great. I really like what you've done."

"Thanks." They'd been redecorating in preparation for the summer clearance sale, and though it did look rather nice, Marisa was surprised Julia had noticed at all. "What brings you here?"

Julia walked over to the counter and set her purse down. "Your father is out of town for the weekend on business, and I thought maybe I could take you out to dinner. I would really like the chance for us to get to know each other before the wedding."

"Lucy and I have plans this evening."

Julia's face crumbled, but she quickly pasted on a cheerful smile. "Well, maybe another time."

She reached for her bag, but Marisa folded a hand over hers and did something she was sure she would later regret. "Why don't you come with us?"

Julia hesitated. "Oh, I don't want to intrude."

"It won't be an intrusion," Lucy piped in. "We're

just going to the bar down the street to see Jake play. We have room for one more at the table.''

"If you're sure it's okay.'' Julia glanced at Marisa.

"It'll be fun. As long as you like jazz.''

Julia nodded enthusiastically. "I love jazz.''

Marisa looked at her watch. "We'll be closing up in about twenty minutes and heading down the street. You can just hang out here until we go.''

"I'd like that.'' She smoothed the skirt of her dress and combed her hair with her fingers. "I'm a little rumpled from the heat. Is there someplace I can freshen my makeup?''

"There's a bathroom in the back, but the lighting is pretty bad. If you want you can use my apartment bathroom. The door is unlocked.''

Marisa showed Julia through the inventory room to the back stairs. When she returned, Lucy was cashing out the register.

"I was all set not to like her,'' Lucy said. "But she seems okay, and very eager to please. It was nice of you to invite her to come with us.''

"I was afraid she would burst into tears if I didn't. I suppose it won't kill me to get to know her a little. It'll make things less awkward at the wedding.''

"Maybe you guys will become friends.''

Marisa didn't bother telling Lucy how unlikely that would be. Joseph's wives were never around long enough for a lasting relationship so she made it a habit not to befriend them. Not that any had tried before now. Most considered her an unfortunate coincidence of his previous life and certainly not worth their time. She had been a support check the third week of every month or a college tuition bill. She'd never been treated like a person.

It was commendable that Julia was making an effort, but Marisa was sure that after the wedding she would make herself plenty scarce.

Eight

"**M**r. Carmichael? Could I, um, get your autograph?"

Jake turned to the young girl standing below him next to the stage, and found himself gazing—*hello*—right down the front of a scoop-neck top. It was a groupie trick—one he'd seen a million times before.

"Sure," he said, hopping down from the stage, taking the pen she held out for him.

She eased down the front of her top to expose a hot pink bra cup, her glossy red lips curving into an inviting smile. "Do you mind?"

He shrugged. He'd signed stranger things in his career. At least this one didn't ask him to sign her bare breast, although, if she had, it wouldn't have been a first.

He scrawled his name across the lacy cup covering her generous left breast then handed the pen back. "There you go."

"I bought this bra at your girlfriend's store," she said, straightening her top. "She's really nice."

"My girlfriend? You mean, Marisa?"

"The one who owns the lingerie shop." She grinned conspiratorially. "I guess technically she's not really your *girlfriend.*"

"I'm sorry, I'm not following you."

"She told me and my best friend about your little secret."

Jake felt as if he'd been punched in the stomach. "She *told* you?"

Why would Marisa do something like that? Hadn't they made up rules? Hadn't they agreed to keep this a secret? Now she was telling virtual strangers?

"Don't worry," the girl said. "We won't tell no one."

He shook his head, still unable to believe it. They had promised. She had never broken a promise. "Marisa actually *told* you what we're doing?"

"Well, it was her friend, the one with the red hair. But Marisa was standing right there."

Lucy knew, too? Who else had she told?

"I'm sorry," the girl said, looking around uneasily. "I didn't mean to get no one in trouble. I just wanted to say congratulations."

Something made Jake turn and glance toward the door. He wasn't surprised to see that Marisa had just walked through. He seemed to have some weird kind of radar these days, knowing instinctively when she entered a room. She was headed toward her regular table, followed by Lucy and Julia.

He turned to say something to the girl, but she was already gone, and he seriously doubted she would be back. He turned back to Marisa's table. How could she do this to him? He'd trusted her. Didn't she understand it was in the kid's best interest not to know who his real father was? The way she was flapping her jaws, pretty soon everyone would know. There would be no way to keep it from the baby.

Marisa smiled at him through the hazy light. Her smile faded when she saw the look on his face.

She shot a few words in Lucy and Julia's direction, her eyes never leaving his, then got up and crossed the bar to meet him. "What's wrong? You look upset."

He took her arm and pulled her to the side of the stage, behind the speakers. "How many people have you told?"

"Told what?"

"About what we've been doing."

"We agreed not to tell anyone. Julia suspects something, but she promised not to say anything."

"Then why did some customer of yours just come up to me and say she knows all about our 'little secret'?"

"I have no idea. Jake, I haven't told anyone."

"Then how did Lucy find out?"

"Lucy doesn't know anything about this. And if she does, she didn't hear it from me."

"This girl said Lucy told her and you were standing right there, So Lucy must know."

Marisa shrugged helplessly.

"Don't tell me you don't remember her—young, cute. She bought a pink bra."

Pink bra? The fog in Marisa's brain began to dissipate. "Was it a hot pink push-up bra?"

"That's the one. She made me autograph the damned thing."

Bra-girl. She should have known. Marisa closed her

eyes and shook her head. "I swear, I'm really going to kill Lucy this time."

"So you did tell her!" He looked more hurt than angry. "Marisa, we agreed not to tell *anyone*. It was a promise. I can't believe you would do this."

She laid a hand on his arm, felt him tense. "I haven't told anyone, and that girl was talking about a different 'little secret.'"

Jake frowned. "Since when do we have more than one?"

"Since Lucy told them that you and I are engaged. It was a joke," she added quickly, so he wouldn't get the wrong idea. "You know how she likes to mess with people. She thought it would be funny. You and I hadn't even talked about the baby stuff at that point."

"So, it was all a joke?"

"You know Lucy and her whacked-out sense of—" She gasped as Jake wrapped his arms around her and pulled her into a bone-crushing embrace.

"I am so sorry," he said, pressing his cheek to her hair. "I should have trusted you."

"Jake, it's okay." She slipped her arms around him, flattening her hands against his back, enjoying the warm, solid muscle. Enjoying it too much. "It was a misunderstanding. It happens."

"I shouldn't have raised my voice to you." His breath was warm on her neck, sending a swarm of tiny shivers across her skin.

Oh, man this felt way too good. Closing her eyes, she inhaled the scent of his hair, his cologne. His arms tightened around her and she sighed, sinking deeper into him. As if possessed, her hands took on a will of their own. They slid down his back, cupped his rear end.

She must have been possessed. She would never do

anything so bold. Especially not in a dark, secluded corner of a bar. But it was definitely her. It was her hands groping him through the fabric of his pants, pulling him closer, until she could feel his hard length against her stomach.

Jake groaned softly and fisted her shirt in both hands. She could feel the conflict, feel him fighting for control. She burrowed her hands under his shirt, dragging her fingernails across his bare skin—

Someone cleared his throat behind them. Jake pushed her away so hard she stumbled backward.

Louis stood on the stage above them. "Uh, sorry, I didn't mean to interrupt."

Jake shoved a hand through his hair. "We were just…it was nothing."

Nothing? Yes, she was nowhere near to ovulating, and yes, she had no right to touch him that way. She even understood his knee-jerk reaction when Louis interrupted them. But to hear the words, to hear him say it was *nothing*.

Louis looked nervously at them. "We're, uh, ready to start."

"I'll be there in a second." He waited until Louis had disappeared, then turned to her. "Marisa, I—"

She threw up a hand to stop him. "Don't say anything. I'm sorry. It was my fault, and it won't happen again."

Before he could agree, or even worse, thank her, she hurried away—feeling as if someone had just ripped her heart from her chest and stomped all over it.

"Jake is amazing!" Julia gushed, gesturing to the waitress for a second ginger ale, confirming Marisa's suspicion that she probably wasn't old enough to drink alcohol. "Are all of the songs original?"

"Most of them," Marisa shouted over the music, keeping her eye on the blonde two tables over—the same blonde who had been hanging out in the bar for weeks now. The way she gazed up at Jake with what Marisa was sure were deep blue eyes—natural blue of course—was a little sickening. No, it was *very* sickening. Gag-me-with-a-fork sickening.

She was tall, gorgeous and leggy. Everything Marisa wasn't.

The blonde had taken a seat right up front and, since he'd begun playing, hadn't taken her eyes off Jake. He didn't typically go for the groupie types, but he appeared awfully distracted by this one. So distracted in fact, that he hadn't even talked to Marisa after the first set.

No wonder he'd been so upset with her earlier that evening. He'd probably been afraid his new girlfriend would find out what was going on between him and Marisa. Maybe that was why he'd been so freaked out when he thought Marisa was telling people about their arrangement. Maybe things with the blonde were getting serious.

"What university did Jake attend?" Julia asked.

"He didn't."

She leaned closer to hear her over the blustery timbre of a trumpet solo. "He studied privately?"

"Real private. All by himself."

Julia's eyes widened. "But, he's incredible! He must have studied with *someone*."

"Jake is immensely gifted."

The set ended and the blonde flew from her seat, clapping enthusiastically, rushing over to meet Jake as he exited the stage and fought his way through a throng of young women.

"Is he signed with a record company?" Julia asked.

"He started his own label. He and the other guys in the band do studio work to keep it going. Jake is one of the most sought after studio musicians in Detroit."

"Who is that woman with him," Lucy asked, eyeing the blonde suspiciously. "The one with the bad dye job. She's been hanging around a lot lately."

Marisa shrugged, trying her best to look indifferent. Not that she had any right to feel threatened or jealous. She had no claim on his affections. "I've never met her. If he's seeing her, he hasn't mentioned it to me."

Marisa felt a tap on her shoulder and turned, surprised to see an unfamiliar man standing behind her.

"Wanna dance?" he asked, flashing a slightly inebriated grin.

Dance? How long had it been since she had danced with anyone besides Jake? Men asked, but she usually said no. But this guy was kind of cute and reasonably well dressed. She couldn't see the harm in one little dance, even if he was obviously intoxicated. When she glanced over and saw Jake watching her, the thought became that much more appealing. She wanted him to see that she, too, could act as if nothing had changed between them. Because it hadn't. He'd made that abundantly clear.

"Go for it," Lucy whispered, jabbing her with her elbow.

"Why not?" she said, rising from her seat. As the man led her to the dance floor, Lucy hooted and Julia gave a low whistle. When she looked over to see Jake's reaction, he was talking with the blonde again.

"Name's Mark," the man said, drawing her into his

arms and pulling her just a wee bit too close for comfort. Either he was getting fresh with her, or he needed the support to keep from falling over. "I've been watching you all night. You're the most beautiful woman I've ever laid eyes on."

"Um, thank you." As far as pickup lines went, it was pretty lame, but she was flattered. At least he cared enough to *try* to pick her up.

He made idle small talk while they danced, which he did surprisingly well considering the overpowering scent of liquor on his breath. He claimed to be an engineer from Chicago, in town on business. When she told him she owned a lingerie shop he looked intrigued, and maybe it was her imagination, but she could swear he was getting a little, um…turned-on.

All the while, she was sure she felt Jake's eyes on her, but each time she looked over he was concentrating on the blonde. Not that he *should* be watching her. Why would he care if she was dancing with another man?

When the song ended, she extricated herself from Mark's arms. "Thanks for the dance."

"Aw, come on, baby. One more," he said, reaching for her. Again she had the sneaking suspicion she was being watched. She looked over at Jake just in time to see him look away. So, he *had* been watching her.

She turned to Mark and smiled, even though he'd had the nerve to call her something as degrading as "baby." "One more."

He locked his arms around her waist and they swayed to the sultry music. She found herself getting a backache as she fought to keep his grinding pelvis a respectable distance away. When his hands slid down to grope her behind, it was the last straw. She planted her palms firmly on his chest and shoved him back.

"Thanks for the dance, Mark. It's been swell." Before he could protest, she spun away from him and wound her way across the crowded dance floor to the ladies' room. The dancing was okay, but the groping didn't do a thing for her. Her new attitude about her body apparently hadn't swayed her views on touchy-feely drunks out for a cheap thrill. Or perhaps her new attitude only applied when the touchy-feely man in question was Jake.

It's just as well, she thought. After she got pregnant and had the baby she wouldn't have time for men.

She used the bathroom then checked her hair and makeup. As she pushed out the door, a large hand wrapped roughly around her arm and pulled her down the back hall.

The air exploded from her lungs as she was crushed to the wall between the phone and the back exit. She barely had time to catch her breath before her captor, who she now realized was Mark-the-Groper, locked his mouth over hers and shoved his tongue down her throat. The overpowering taste of alcohol was enough to give her a contact buzz.

Isn't this special? she thought, as she pried her mouth away. Maybe dancing with him hadn't been such a hot idea after all. He'd looked harmless enough.

"Whatsa matter," he slurred, pressing her to the wall with his body. Apparently the alcohol hadn't affected certain protruding parts of his anatomy. Unfortunately for him, when he'd pinned her, she had strategically shifted her leg between his two. It would take only one solid blow and the guy would be toast. Out of fairness, she would give him the chance to surrender under his own free will.

"I want to take you home tonight, baby."

"If I gave you the impression I was interested in anything other than a dance, that wasn't my intention. I'd appreciate it if you'd let me go. *Now*."

He reached up to grope her left breast.

She'd warned him. Grabbing his shoulders to center her balance and add momentum to the thrust, she was about to let her knee fly, when suddenly he was jerked backward and flung into the opposite wall.

Jake stood in the hallway, fists clenched, his eyes wild with rage. "I believe the lady asked you to let go."

The whole scene was eerily reminiscent of the day they'd met, when two eighth-grade boys had cornered her outside the school and, in graphic language, told her exactly what they intended to do to her. Anyone who knew of her mother—and most adolescent boys had heard a thing or two about the neighborhood tramp— figured the apple didn't fall far from the tree. Then Jake Carmichael, younger brother of the bad boy Tom Carmichael, had come along and at eleven years old had looked threatening enough to scare off two thirteen-year-olds without raising a finger.

But that had been different. She had been a scared little girl overpowered by boys nearly twice her size. She was a grown woman now with the skills to fight off a slobbering drunk.

Mark-the-Groper slid to the ground by the men's room door and Jake hovered menacingly over him. "Beat it," he barked, and the guy wasted no time scrambling away, mumbling slurred apologies.

"Jake! What do you think you're doing?" she snapped.

"Saving you," Jake said, grabbing her arm, hastily looking her up and down. "Did he hurt you?"

"Saving me? Who said I needed saving."

He stared at her incredulously. "That creep was all over you. Don't tell me you actually wanted him molesting you."

She ripped her arm free. "Of course I didn't. I had it under control."

He let out a bark of a laugh. "Yeah, you really looked like you were in control of the situation when his tongue was in your mouth."

"You macho jerk! I am not a helpless little girl anymore. I don't need big bad Jake Carmichael to protect me." Shoving the back door open, she hurled herself into the alley and stomped away.

Nine

Jake followed Marisa out the door, still fuming that she would dance with that creep in the first place. The thought of someone hurting her, of another man's hands on her, hit him like a blow to the gut. "Didn't you notice that the guy was plastered when he asked you to dance? Did you want him pawing you like that? Did you enjoy it?"

She stopped dead and looked back at him with a glare that could have singed off his eyebrows, and he realized what he'd implied. Before he could take it back, she was stalking away.

He went after her. "Marisa, wait. That's not what I meant. Where are you going?"

She wouldn't even look at him.

"Home," she ground out through clenched teeth. "And don't you dare follow me."

"It's dark and you're in an alley. You're damn right I'm going to follow you."

"Go back to your girlfriend, Jake."

"Girlfriend?" He reached for her arm, clamping his fingers around her wrist. "Marisa, slow down!"

She ripped her arm away. "Don't manhandle me!"

"Manhandle?"

She crossed her arms over her chest. "For your information, I could have taken care of myself just fine back there. I took self-defense courses in college. I'm more than capable of defending myself."

Self-defense courses? Jake felt like a first-rate jerk. He'd gone in like gangbusters ready to rescue her, and he hadn't even stopped to consider that she didn't need his help. Then he'd turned it around and made it sound as though it was her fault, as though she'd asked for it.

Even worse, he'd lost his temper. For the second time that night. It was time he faced the truth. Marisa didn't need him watching over her anymore.

The thought made him feel hollow inside. Marisa had always needed him. Hell, who would he be if he wasn't Marisa's keeper, her bodyguard? Had that just been an illusion? What if there came a time when she didn't need his friendship, either? What would he do then?

"I'm sorry," he said, stuffing his hands in his pockets. "When I saw that guy all over you, and thought of him hurting you, I just went crazy."

"How did you even know we were back there?"

"When I saw him follow you to the bathroom, I knew something was up." The alley was dark, but he could see the hint of a smile on her face. "I guess I overreacted a little."

"A little," she agreed. "It's kinda sweet that you still feel the need to protect me. Annoying, but sweet."

"I'm sorry for what I said. I didn't mean it. I know you're not like your mother."

"I know that, too. It took me a while to figure it out, but I think it's finally sinking in."

"If you're leaving, would you at least let me walk you home?"

"What about the blonde?"

"What blonde?"

She avoided his eyes. "You know, the one you've been hanging around with. Won't she wonder where you went?"

She was jealous. He almost laughed as relief gushed up inside of him. That meant she had probably only danced with that creep to make *him* jealous in return. And it had worked. He'd been ready to spit nails when he saw her dancing with that guy. When he so much as thought of her in anyone's arms but his own. "Don't worry about her. She'll understand."

They started down the alley toward the street. "Two fights in one night," she said. "I think that's a first for us."

"I think you're right." He pulled his hand out of his pocket and laced his fingers through hers. Her skin was soft and warm, her grip firm as she squeezed his hand. He felt it in a hot rush that started in his face and shot straight down to his toes. He'd heard of people becoming aroused by anger, but he'd never believed it.

Until now.

It couldn't be a coincidence when it happened twice in one evening. If Louis hadn't interrupted them earlier, he might not have been able to stop himself. He'd have taken her right there next to the stage, behind the speaker.

But that was against the rules. He couldn't touch her

until she ovulated and God only knows when that would happen. He'd been making an effort lately to keep a safe physical distance. He enjoyed making love with her—enjoyed it far too much—and thought about it far too often. He'd even thought about crazy things, like making this arrangement permanent. Good friends who sleep together when the mood hits them, no strings attached. And the mood seemed to be hitting them both an awful lot lately, hadn't it?

But Marisa and his baby deserved better than that. Better than him, anyway.

"As fights go, I'd say it was a pretty good one," she offered.

He nodded. His grip on her hand tightened and she looked up at him, a question in her eyes. Before he knew what he was doing, he had her pinned to the nearest telephone pole. His mouth came down hard and swift on hers, his tongue thrusting to taste her. It would have served him right if she'd hauled off and punched him, but she didn't. She wound her fingers through his hair, pulling him closer. Then her hands seemed to be everywhere at once—sliding under his shirt, raking over his chest and back.

He grasped her skirt and yanked it up. She eased her thighs apart, moaning into his mouth as he filled his hands with the smooth rounded flesh of her behind. He echoed her with a moan of his own when he felt her stroking him through his jeans.

It wasn't enough. He wanted her naked, he needed to be inside her. But, not here, not in the alley.

The alley?

What was he doing? What were *they* doing? Realization hit simultaneously and they tore themselves away from each other, both gasping for breath.

"Well," she said, straightening her skirt. "That was…unexpected."

Jake cleared his throat. "I guess we almost broke a rule."

"Yes, I noticed that, too." She avoided his eyes, glanced nervously up and down the alley, probably to make sure no one had seen. "It must have been the margaritas."

The margaritas? The first time, beside the stage, she hadn't even had a drink yet! Couldn't she just admit that it was a moment of weakness on both their parts? Repressed lust gone awry. Or was it too much to admit that she would stoop so low as to lust after him? He was good enough to impregnate her but not quite up to snuff for any kind of lasting physical relationship?

Lasting physical relationship? Where was he getting this garbage? He didn't want a lasting anything with anyone that was even remotely physical.

"I think I should go home now," she said.

"I'll walk you."

She hesitated. "Um, maybe you shouldn't."

"Don't worry, I'm not coming up. I'll drop you off at your door and leave. How much damage can we do on a crowded sidewalk?"

A police car with its sirens wailing flew past, sending flashes of red and blue light across the shadows of her face. "Maybe I should tell Lucy and Julia I'm leaving."

"I'll tell them when I get back." He held out a hand for her to take. "Come on."

She looked at his hand for a second, then slipped her fingers through his. They walked in silence to the street. "Jake," she said softly. "It wasn't the margaritas."

He squeezed her hand as emotion took a stubborn hold on his heart and wouldn't let go. "I know."

A fire engine sped past, then another. As they turned the corner an ambulance joined the company of flashing lights several blocks down the street.

''I wonder what happened,'' Marisa said as another police cruiser shot past.

Jake craned his neck to see over the crowds gathering on the sidewalk. Those emergency vehicles were stopped awfully close to…no, it couldn't be. ''Marisa, that's not—''

She had already let go of his hand and was shoving her way through the ocean of bodies clogging the sidewalk. Against a backdrop of blackness, billows of gray smoke hung ominously in the moonlit sky.

Right over Marisa's building.

It could be worse.

That seemed to be the consensus as Marisa leaned on the back of the police cruiser, watching the firemen pack up their gear. She supposed that was pretty easy to say when you hadn't just lost *everything* you owned. When your business—your livelihood—hadn't just burned up.

''Miss Donato?''

Marisa looked up to see Annie, Mr. Kloppman's daughter. They'd taken her father away by ambulance shortly after Marisa and Jake had arrived to find the upper half of the building consumed by flames and billowing smoke.

Her face was streaked with tears. ''Miss Donato, I'm so very sorry for what's happened.''

''Is your father okay?''

She nodded, wiping her cheeks. ''He's got a few second-degree burns and suffered from mild smoke inhalation.''

"I'm glad he'll be all right." Marisa rubbed her eyes with her thumb and forefinger. They burned from sheer exhaustion and the acrid smoke still hanging in the air. All she wanted to do was crawl into bed and sleep, but she didn't have a bed to crawl into anymore. She didn't even have clean clothes to change into, or a toothbrush. She had nothing.

"This is all my fault," Annie hiccuped, fresh tears springing from her eyes. "I knew he wasn't well, but he wanted to be independent. I couldn't bear putting him in a home. He was so happy here."

"Did he say why he did it?"

"He wasn't making much sense. He mumbled something about a strange girl. She wouldn't let him scan her, so he was convinced she was an alien or a spy or something. When she came back tonight, he thought she was after him and panicked. He said he was burning 'documents.' He kept files and files full of newspaper clippings and things he'd printed off the Internet. In his mind, they were important."

Marisa looked over at Julia, who stood huddled with Lucy and Jake on the sidewalk speaking to one of the police officers. Mr. Kloppman had set the building on fire because he thought her father's fiancée was an alien. How absolutely perfect. She would have laughed, but she didn't have the energy left. She didn't even have the energy to cry.

"I'm so sorry," Annie said again. "All of your things, your beautiful store—"

"They're just things," she assured her. "They can be replaced. People can't. All that matters is everyone is okay. You should go and be with your dad. He needs you."

Annie reluctantly left and Marisa watched her walk

away, feeling only pity. Mr. Kloppman wasn't malicious and she truly believed he never meant to harm anyone. He'd been a good, if not entertaining tenant for six years. Now Annie would have no choice but to put him in a nursing home, or possibly institutionalize him.

Jake sat next to her on the trunk, wrapping an arm around her shoulders. They both smelled like barbecued carpet and their clothes were damp and dirty. "You holding up okay?"

No, she wasn't okay. She was exhausted and depressed and homeless. She nodded anyway. "Don't you have to go back to the bar?"

"I called Louis and explained the situation. I'm not going anywhere." The arm around her tightened. Now came the bad news.

"A building inspector will be out in the morning. When he says it's safe, we can go in and pick up whatever wasn't ruined. Lucy called your insurance company and they're sending an adjuster out when they get the all clear."

"Did the firemen say how bad it is?"

"Mr. Kloppman's place, the hallway and everything below are going to have to be gutted. Most of the fire was contained to that part of the building. Your living room is singed, but it was superficial. Most of the damage is going to be from smoke and water."

She stifled a yawn and rubbed the sleep from her eyes. Now that all of the emergency vehicles were pulling away, the crowds on the sidewalks had thinned to a few stragglers. She was beginning to feel less like a circus sideshow.

Julia and Lucy joined them in the street.

"Is she okay?" Julia asked Jake.

"She's fine," Marisa answered for him. "She's just exhausted."

"Come home with me," Julia said. "You can stay with me and your father."

"You're welcome to stay with me and my grandma," Lucy offered.

Before Marisa could accept or refuse either of their offers, Jake stood, pulling her with him. "She's staying with me."

I am? she almost said. She didn't remember him asking. Although, she couldn't imagine another place she would rather stay, where she would feel more comfortable, and less like a charity case.

"There's no point in hanging around here anymore," he said. "Let's go home."

Home? She didn't have a home. But she didn't bother to point that out.

"I'll help you pack up your stuff," Lucy promised. "Call me."

"Me, too," Julia said, pulling Marisa into a firm embrace. "Anything you need, I'm only a phone call away."

Marisa thanked them and let Jake lead her to his Jeep in the public parking lot two blocks away. He unlocked the door for her, helped her in and fastened her seat belt. She wasn't much in the mood for conversation, so she sat quietly as he drove to his place, a small, converted warehouse on the other side of town. He found a parking spot around the corner, helped her out of the Jeep and led her inside.

The building was old and drafty and needed a lot of work, but it was large enough to hold band practice and he never had to worry about the music disturbing his neighbors. Marisa had always thought it suited his personality. Open and honest and maybe a little rough around the edges—what you saw was what you got.

Besides the bathroom, the apartment was one big open area with a louvered privacy screen separating the bedroom from the rest of the space. The furniture was mismatched but comfortably casual. Most of the pieces they had picked out together at estate and garage sales. Like her own apartment, it wasn't a disaster, but there was always a healthy level of clutter.

Locking the door behind them, Jake tossed his keys on the coffee table and kicked off his shoes. "You can have my room, I'll sleep on the sofa bed."

"I'm not kicking you out of your bed, Jake. I'll take the sofa. And don't try to argue," she said when he opened his mouth to object.

"Are you hungry?"

She slid her sandals off. "No, but I could use a bath. And some clean clothes."

"Everything you need should be in the bathroom, and I think there's a spare toothbrush in the closet. I'll find you something to wear and fix up the couch."

Marisa disappeared into the bathroom and a moment later Jake heard the water running. He wished there was something he could do or say to make this easier for her, to make it all better. He'd always felt that way when his dad went after his mom—useless, helpless. He had tried once to intervene, and had gotten a fractured rib for his trouble. His mom had begged him never to interfere again.

"It was my fault," she'd whispered, even though the old man was passed out cold in front of the television. "I shouldn't have raised my voice. He's my husband. I should show him respect."

"He shouldn't hit us," Jake had said.

His mother hugged him then, which she hadn't done very often because his father would only get angry and call him a sissy. Her fat lip had felt hot against Jake's cheek. "He can't help it, baby. It's just in his nature. You'll understand when you get older."

He shook his head. "I would never hit a woman. I would never hurt anyone."

She'd held him at arm's length. "My father did, and his father before him. It's in your blood, Jake—in the genes. It's a curse. Do yourself a favor and never get married, or you'll be just like them."

He hadn't believed her. Not until Tommy—his hero—had gone off the deep end. Then he knew it was true. And he knew it would happen to him, too, if he wasn't careful. So he'd taken his mother's advice to heart.

Jake pulled out the sofa bed, and after brushing it free of stray popcorn kernels and spare change, he spread fresh sheets on. Next he rifled through the basket of clean clothes on his bedroom floor until he found a T-shirt and a pair of drawstring jogging shorts he thought might fit her.

"I have some clothes for you," he called through the bathroom door.

"Come in," she replied.

Jake paused, his hand on the knob. She was naked in there, he reminded himself, and as rotten as the evening had been, he was still human. He dropped the clothes inside the door and turned to leave. "Here you go."

"Keep me company for a minute?" she called.

He swore silently. "Uh, sure."

He opened the door wider and stepped into the bathroom, relieved to see that she was submerged to the chin in the deep, claw-foot tub. A mountain of frothy bubbles shielded her nudity.

"You're okay with this?" she asked, looking up at him with bloodshot brown eyes. "I don't want to make you uncomfortable."

A smile tugged at his mouth. "I think we're safe until the bubbles evaporate. Where did they come from anyway? I can't remember ever taking a bubble bath."

"Shampoo. It works in a pinch." Her nose twitched with distaste. "I washed my hair twice and it still smells like smoke."

Though it was against his better judgment, he crouched down on the floor next to the tub and grabbed the bottle of shampoo. Squeezing out a handful, he massaged it into her hair, starting at the scalp and working his way down.

"That feels nice." She sighed, resting her head against the edge of the tub.

It would be so easy to lean forward and kiss her. Her mouth was so close, so full and inviting. When her tongue slipped out to wet her lips, he had to look away.

"You know, we're breaking rule number..." She paused, her brow crinkling. "Actually, I don't remember which number it is because the list is back in my apartment. But we're not supposed to do sleepovers."

"Consider this extenuating circumstances. Besides, if we're in separate beds, it doesn't count. Sit up."

She sat forward, drawing her knees up to her chest. He used the plastic cup by the sink to rinse her hair, running his fingers through the silky strands. She closed her eyes and leaned her head back. Her mouth was so close, her lips so lush and kissable...

His groin tightened with sudden, intense arousal.

"We're roommates until your apartment is livable,"

he said. He could handle that. Sure he could. He would just take a lot of cold showers.

He'd need a really long one tonight.

"I can't put you out like that. The insurance will pay for a hotel."

"Forget it. I won't let you spend months in a hotel. I've done it and it sucks." He poured one last cup of water over her hair. "Done."

"Thanks." She glanced up at him, her nose wrinkled. "I hate to say it, but you stink."

"Thanks a lot." He splashed her playfully and got an honest-to-goodness smile. He dried his hands on a towel and pulled himself to his feet. It was going on one in the morning, and though he was accustomed to staying up late, he was bushed. It had been one hell of a long night. "I guess I probably could use a shower."

"Give me two minutes and I'll be out of here."

"No rush." He started out the door, hoping she didn't notice the conspicuous tent in the front of his pants.

"Jake?"

He stopped, shielding the front of his body with the door. "Huh?"

"Thanks. For everything."

"My pleasure," he said, knowing that was the understatement of the year.

Marisa curled up under the sheet on the sofa bed, listening to the hiss of the shower, and the intermittent slap of water against the porcelain tub as Jake moved beneath the spray. Though she was exhausted beyond comprehension, sleep still evaded her. She'd spent the night in Jake's apartment before. When she'd had the wood floors in her apartment refinished she'd stayed for three whole days and hadn't felt restless at all. Why was tonight so different?

The water shut off and she heard the sound of the shower curtain opening. She heard Jake brushing his teeth, heard the toilet flush, then the bathroom door opened. The streetlights outside cast a faint glow through the window shades and she could see his silhouette as he padded across the floor to his bedroom. The bed squeaked softly when he climbed in, and the covers rustled as he got comfortable. Then the apartment was quiet.

Too quiet.

He'd been so wonderful tonight, taking care of her, pampering her. He would get her though this, just like when they were kids. She remembered nights when her mother hadn't come home, nights when she'd been scared and alone. Jake would sneak out his bedroom window and come to her house, curl up in her bed and hold her. It had been so long ago, but she realized suddenly that she missed that.

She flung the sheet off and climbed out of bed. The room was warm, bordering on uncomfortable, but the scarred wood floor felt cool beneath her bare feet. Jake lay on his back in bed, the sheet pulled to his waist, both hands tucked under his head. As she stepped closer, she realized his eyes were open.

"Can't sleep?" he asked, and she shook her head. He pulled the sheet back, inviting her in. She didn't even have to ask. He knew just what to do.

She climbed in and he held an arm out, the way he used to, so she curled against him, resting her head on his chest. He smelled clean, like soap.

"Are we breaking the rule now?" she asked sleepily.

"Nope, as long as we keep our clothes on, we're

okay," he said, stroking her still-damp hair. "Close your eyes."

Her lids suddenly felt like lead weights, and she let them close. She was safe now. Nothing could hurt her when she was in Jake's arms.

Ten

Marisa stared up into the gaping hole in the ceiling of the stockroom, where Mr. Kloppman's floor used to be. She couldn't believe this was happening to her—that everything she'd worked so hard for stood in ruins. Temporarily, she reminded herself. It was fixable. Her life would be back on track. It would just take time.

Yellow caution tape blocked off half of the stockroom and the door to Mr. Kloppman's apartment upstairs. Her own apartment, singed as it was, was still accessible. Not that much of it was worth saving. They'd stopped the fire before it reached the kitchen, but the excessive heat had melted anything made of plastic, and the ceiling was black with soot. Even the clothes tucked away in her closet, far from the reaches of the flames, reeked with the stench of stale smoke. She, Jake and Lucy had packed her clothes in black trash bags and Julia had hauled them to a dry cleaner that specialized in removing the smoke smell from fabric.

Despite Lucy's offer to lend her some clothes, Marisa settled for the T-shirt and shorts Jake had loaned her last night. There was something about wearing his clothes that, when she stopped to think about it, made her feel giddy, like a high-school girl wearing her boyfriend's letter jacket. She tried not to think about it. It didn't make any sense. She wasn't in high school, he didn't even own a letter jacket, and she wasn't his girlfriend in the first place.

Behind her, Jake's footsteps landed heavy on the stairs as he descended, a cardboard box balanced in his arms. With the afternoon temperature up near the nineties, and the air-conditioning temporarily out of service, he'd peeled his shirt off hours ago. Marisa put aside her inane musings momentarily to admire the muscles bunching and flexing in his arms and shoulders. She tried to forget how good those arms had felt around her last night. How safe they made her feel. She also tried to ignore the little tingles those muscles were making her feel now.

Despite what had happened in the alley last night, there had been nothing at all sexual about them sleeping in the same bed. It had been so completely nonsexual, she had to wonder if what had transpired earlier had been some fluke of nature. The look he'd gotten in his eyes, she could have sworn he would eat her alive. It hadn't taken much for him to shut those urges out. And if he could block them out, then so could she.

And she would start by not looking at his muscles.

Julia came down a moment later with another box. She'd pulled her hair back in a ponytail and, like Jake's jeans, her clothes were damp and smudged with soot.

Marisa never imagined her looking so unkempt, but it suited her somehow. Maybe it made her seem more human, and less the trophy wife Marisa had thought she would be. Though she kept trying to fight it, she liked Julia.

"That's the rest of the dishes," Jake said. "I'll put these last two boxes in the truck and take everything over to the storage place."

"I boxed up all of the photo albums and books on the shelf in your bedroom closet," Julia said as he took the box from her and headed out. "They didn't seem to smell too bad, but it's hard to tell. I'm immune to it."

Normally it would have bothered her to have a virtual stranger rifling through her personal things, but Marisa felt only gratitude. Julia was the last person on earth she would have expected to come through for her in an emergency. It was becoming clear to her that Julia truly wanted to be her friend, and not out of some warped sense of familial obligation. "Thanks for helping out," she said. "It means a lot to me."

"I spoke to your father this morning. He'll be home tonight. He figured you probably won't accept his help, but he wants you to know that he's there for you if you need him."

"I should have a check from the insurance company on Monday for my living expenses and they'll find a contractor to rebuild. Pretty much everything is covered."

"Just so you know that he's there, and he wants to help. And not just financially."

Marisa wished she could believe that. She wished it wasn't Julia putting words into his mouth. Financially had been the only way Joseph had ever been there for her, and that was only because the courts had ordered him to be.

"I'll keep that in mind," she said, but she could tell Julia didn't believe it. Rather than explain her skepticism, she changed the subject. "Are you coming to Jake's for pizza? The least we can do for all of your help is feed you."

"Did I hear someone say something about food?" Lucy came down the stairs, a box in her arms. As usual, her hair was a mess of curls all flopping in her face. "Kitchen drawers are empty."

"Thanks, Luce." Marisa reached for the box. "I'll take this out to the truck."

Lucy hesitated, glancing at Julia. "Actually, I was wondering if I could talk to you for a minute."

Julia took the hint. "Why don't I carry this out before Jake leaves," she said, taking the box from Lucy. "Maybe I'll go with him and help unload."

"What's the big secret," Marisa asked when Julia was gone.

Lucy reached into her pocket and pulled out a folded sheet of paper. "I found this in the kitchen drawer."

Marisa unfolded the paper and started reading.

"'One—total honesty. Two—only make love during ovulation.'"

She closed her eyes. Oh dammit.

Oh dammit.

"Thought you might like to keep it handy," she said, looking smug. "It seemed pretty important."

"There's a perfectly logical explanation for this," Marisa said.

"It's not as if I didn't already suspect something was going on with you two. You're not exactly quiet, if you know what I mean."

Marisa's heart lodged somewhere near her spleen. "Q-quiet?"

"The day you went up for your *nap*. I was dusting the display in the front window and I saw Jake go up the stairs. I thought it was kind of weird that he didn't come through the store, but I forgot about it after a few minutes. Then I heard the, uh, *noise*."

Marisa bit her lip. "Noise?"

"Your bedroom is directly above the front display, and you know these old buildings. They aren't exactly soundproof. Voices travel through the vents, and, well, you were kind of screaming his name."

"Oh, God." Marisa covered her face with her hands. "You heard that?"

"Marisa, I think half the neighborhood probably heard you. When you didn't say anything about it to me, I kind of figured you guys were just working off some pent-up energy. Like maybe it was a onetime fling you didn't want me to know about. Then I tried to bring it up, the way he's been looking at you, and you laughed it off. I'd forgotten about the whole baby thing. When I saw this, I figured it out."

Marisa dragged both hands over her face. "I am so embarrassed."

"Don't be. Jake must be…whoa. If I had someone who could make me scream like that, I would throw away my toys—"

"Enough!" Marisa said, her cheeks crimson. "I can't believe we're talking about this."

Lucy laughed. "It's nothing to be embarrassed about. It's human nature. Everyone does it." She looked down at the list in Marisa's hand. "Well, everyone but Jake, I guess."

"I am so embarrassed."

"Why? I've been waiting for six years to see you two finally jump each other. Don't even think you're going to walk out of here without giving me some details."

Marisa leaned against the wall, resigned to spilling the beans. What was she so worried about anyway? She knew it wouldn't go any further than this room—or, what was left of this room.

She gave Lucy the abbreviated version of her and Jake's arrangement.

"And now you're living with him," Lucy said with a wistful sigh. "Do you have any idea how much fun you guys could have?"

"As you've probably noticed, rule number two specifically states that we can only make love when I'm ovulating."

"Who said anything about making love? I'm talking about foreplay. The rules say nothing at all about that."

"True, but—"

"There is no but. Look it up in the dictionary. Making love is intercourse. Foreplay is not intercourse."

Lucy definitely had a point. The rules did specifically say "making love." And they wouldn't be making love, so it wouldn't be breaking any rules. Right?

"So, what happens after you get pregnant?" Lucy asked. "Does everything go back to normal? You guys will just be friends again?"

"That's the plan."

"It sounded to me like you and Jake were having a really good time. Doesn't it make sense to enjoy him as often as you can until it's over?"

Another really good point. Two or three weeks more and she could be pregnant. It could be over. "You won't say anything to anyone about this, will you?

About me trying to get pregnant, I mean. We really wanted it to be a secret.''

"My lips are sealed.''

The door clanged open and Julia walked in, cutting their discussion short.

"Jake wants us to meet him at his place so we can order the pizza,'' Julia said, rubbing at a smudge of soot on her arm. "I'd like to go home for a shower first.''

"Nah, don't worry about it,'' Lucy said, draping an arm around Julia's shoulder. "We're all equally dirty and smelly. We'll cancel each other out.'' Lucy turned to Marisa and winked. "Ready to go?''

Marisa took one last look around the store. She still couldn't believe she would be starting from scratch, as she had six years ago. Maybe it was life's way of telling her that she needed a complete makeover. A fresh start.

The coming months would be long and probably frustrating as she rebuilt her life. After she had a baby, her life would change drastically once again. In the meantime, would it kill her, for the first time in her life, to go a little wild and have some fun?

Jake settled on the couch, pushed an empty pizza box out of the way with his toe and propped his feet on the coffee table. With the exception of a few odds and ends and the larger furniture, they had managed to pack Marisa's salvageable belongings and haul them to storage. The rest they would leave to professional movers.

He raked his wet hair back with his fingers and yawned. All of those trips up and down the stairs at Marisa's building had done a number on him physically. He was exhausted and ached from head to toe, but he felt funny going to bed before her. As if it would be rude somehow. Living together, however temporarily, was going to take some getting used to. He was a loner by nature. Even when he'd been out on the road, he never shared rooms with other musicians. He liked his privacy.

With Marisa it was different, of course. They were best friends. He liked spending time with her. He could probably even get used to living with her, if the sex—or lack of it—didn't drive him completely out of his mind.

The bathroom door swung open and he turned to see Marisa emerge on a cloud of steam. At least someone could indulge in a hot shower. He had the bad feeling that, with them living in such close proximity, until she ovulated he was going to be using up an awful lot of cold water.

"I feel so much better." Marisa walked toward the couch, rubbing her hair dry with a towel. Her clothes were still at the cleaners, so she had borrowed another one of his T-shirts and—ah, Lord—she wasn't wearing any pants. He looked away. It was great that she felt comfortable enough to walk around in her underwear. And he couldn't really see anything. Well, nothing besides creamy smooth legs and small, delicate feet with toes tipped hot pink. But it was the idea that she wasn't wearing pants that was turning him on. He wondered what kind of panties she wore underneath. Maybe a thong…

He pulled a throw pillow onto his lap and cursed himself for not taking the time to put a shirt on after his own shower. The thin nylon jogging pants he'd pulled on didn't hide much.

She dropped down on the couch, propping her feet on the table next to his, their thighs touching. "Want to watch a movie or something?"

Or something. Jake swallowed and pressed the pillow a little more firmly into his lap. The heat radiating from her skin seeped through his pant leg. "Actually, I'm pretty beat. I think I'll just go to bed."

She laid a hand on his knee, drawing lazy circles with her thumbnail. "It's only ten-thirty. I've never seen you go to bed before one."

Jake sat mesmerized as her hand inched its way up his thigh. It was a completely innocent move on her part and he felt like a weasel for getting so aroused. Then she drew one knee up to her chin and the T-shirt rode up, exposing a small patch of black underneath.

Black panties. She was wearing silky black panties. He tried to swallow again, but his throat seized. Her hand was still on his leg. Still inching its way up. If he didn't know any better, he would swear she was trying to seduce him. It would be easier to think that than blame this on his own lack of discipline.

Yawning, she clasped her hands over her head and stretched. It was a relief that she'd finally stopped touching him, until he noticed her nipples poking erotically against the fabric of her shirt. Through the faded white cotton he could see the dark outline of each erect peak…

Looking away, he dug his fingers deep into the pillow and gritted his teeth. He had to get off this couch. He had to get away from Marisa *now,* but there was no way he could drop the pillow without her noticing his condition. He would walk away holding the pillow, but even Marisa, innocent as she was, would catch on to that.

"You're awfully quiet," she said. Her hand was back on his leg, on his inner thigh, slowly sliding up.

Maybe they should write a few ground rules for living together. Rule number one, no sitting within ten feet of each other. Rule two, no looking at each other. Rule three, no black silk underwear.

"I'm…" Hot for you. Horny as hell. Dying over here. "…concentrating."

"Concentrating on what?" She was halfway up his thigh now and still going, her touch frustratingly light.

He had two choices. He could take her hand and shove it into his pants, but that would be rather bold and grossly inappropriate considering the situation, or he could be honest with her and put an end to this torture.

Very gently, he took her hand and placed it on her own leg. "Let's just say that it would be in your best interest not to touch me right now."

She looked up at him, her cinnamon eyes wide and innocent. "Are you aroused?"

Aw, hell, now he really felt like a degenerate. "I'm sorry. It's not your fault…well, I guess technically it is your fault, but…" He shrugged helplessly. "What can I say? I'm a guy."

"Let me see."

"You want to see? Marisa, don't—"

Before he could stop her, she tugged the pillow out of his lap. Her eyes widened. "Wow, I guess you are."

He expected her to be appalled by his lack of control. He was sure she would at least get up from the couch. He never expected her mouth to curl into a satisfied, seductive smile.

"It amazes me that something as simple as me touching your leg can have this effect on you."

"You mean, you were doing that on purpose?" He reached for the pillow, but she tossed it over her shoulder.

"You know, Jake, for someone so intelligent, you can be really dense sometimes." She leaned down and pressed a kiss to his bare stomach, just above the waist of his pants and every ounce of blood in his body shot directly to his crotch. Her hair was damp from her shower and felt cold where it touched his skin.

"What are you doing?" he rasped, clutching the arm of the couch. He couldn't muster the resistance to push her away. "You know, we have rules about this kind of thing."

"Nowhere in the rules does it say I can't kiss you." She popped one of the snaps that ran down the leg seam of his pants. "Does it?"

"Well, no, but it says no making love when you're not ovulating."

Her lips brushed lower, below his navel, and he heard the pop of another snap opening. "Who said I want to make love?"

Pop. Her breath, hot and damp against his skin, made his groin throb. If she didn't want to make love, what *did* she want to do?

"We, uh, made that list of rules for a reason. So, so…" His mind went blank when he felt her tongue slide warm and wet across his belly. *Come on, Jake, think. There was a really good reason.*

"So we wouldn't get confused," she finished for him. She sat up, looking him in the eyes, her lush lips inches from his. "Are you confused?"

Confused? She seemed to be speaking a foreign language. They weren't supposed to touch each other until she ovulated. She wasn't supposed to just seduce him. This wasn't like her.

"A little," he squeaked. "I am a little confused."

"Then let me explain. After tonight, it's two weeks of abstinence for you, correct?"

He nodded.

"Okay, then, would you rather do this by yourself, or would it be more fun if I participated?"

The anticipation of how she might participate, particularly things involving her mouth, made his heart pump double time. "Your participation would definitely be more fun, but—"

"I want to make you feel good, and there's nothing in our rules that says I shouldn't. We don't have to make love."

"This won't be confusing for you? You know, emotionally."

"If I weren't so emotionally grounded, I never would have made it through today in one piece. When I was packing up what's left of my stuff, I was realizing how quickly things change. Life is too short to worry about what may or may not affect me emotionally. Pretty soon I'll be pregnant. Why shouldn't we enjoy each other right now, while we can?"

It was hard to argue with logic like that. Of course, as she slid to the floor, tugging his pants down to his ankles, just about any reason would have sounded pretty logical to him. Her T-shirt and panties joined his pants in a pile on the floor. Her breasts, full and soft, pressed against his thighs as she leaned forward.

She seemed to know what she wanted, and any sane man would shut his mouth, close his eyes and enjoy. She was leaning over, licking her lips before she—

A loud rap at the door made them both jolt with surprise.

Marisa snatched her T-shirt off the floor and pulled

it over her head. "It's almost eleven. Who could that be?"

"How should I know?"

"Were you expecting someone?"

"No!" Jake stood up and yanked his pants on, fumbling with the snaps. "I'll go see who it is. But I swear, if it's not the prize patrol here to tell me I've won a million dollars, I'm not opening that door."

Marisa frantically searched the floor. "Where is my underwear?"

He left her groping on her hands and knees for her panties and stomped across the room to the door. He flicked the switch for the front light and looked out the peephole, groaning when he recognized the person on the other side.

Eleven

"Marisa, you're not going to believe this. It's your dad."

"My dad?" What in the world was he doing there? "Keep him busy while I go put some pants on."

"I'm half-naked!"

"Wear this." She peeled the T-shirt off and threw it in his direction, then turned, clutching her panties, and ran naked as a newborn for the bedroom. When she was safely behind the privacy screen, she pulled her panties on and searched frantically for the basket of clothes where she'd tossed her bra and shorts. Then she remembered that she'd left it in the bathroom after her shower.

From the other room she heard the door open and the echo of voices. Oh, special. What was she supposed to do now, streak through the apartment in her underwear? That wouldn't look suspicious. She threw open Jake's closet and latched onto the first thing she saw—a very loud Hawaiian-print shirt. She tugged it off the hanger, knowing not even the bright pattern would hide the fact that she was braless.

No way would the jeans or cargo pants hanging there fit her, so she tried the drawers of the antique bureau. One was filled with sweat socks and briefs, another held silk boxer shorts. The rest of the drawers were empty.

"Marisa," Jake called. "Someone here to see you."

"Be right there!"

Briefs or boxers. Well, that was easy. She chose a pair of plain black boxers and slipped them on. Hopefully Joseph wouldn't notice. They were too large in the waist, so she tucked the edge under her panties to keep them from falling down to her ankles. She glanced around for a mirror to see how utterly ridiculous she looked. Of course, being gorgeous by nature and completely lacking in vanity, he didn't have one.

She didn't need a mirror to know exactly what Joseph would think. He would take one look at her and see her mother.

She fought a sudden stab of resentment. Marisa, you're a grown woman. Why on earth do you care what he thinks? But for some reason, she did. She didn't want him, or anyone else for that matter, to think of her that way.

Taking a deep breath, she stepped out of the bedroom. Jake and Joseph stood close to the door—Jake barefoot, his hair mussed adorably, and Joseph dressed to the nines in a charcoal pinstripe suit. Two men couldn't have looked more different. Although they both looked equally relieved to see her.

"Hello, Joseph," she said, and noticed him not so subtly scan her from head to toe, his brow lifted slightly. Though he'd probably spent the better portion of the day on a plane, nary a wrinkle could be seen on his clothing. The man wasn't human. It had to be ninety degrees outside, and he hadn't even broken a sweat.

"I'll, um, leave you two alone to catch up," Jake said, backing toward the bedroom. "Holler if you need anything."

She didn't blame him for bolting. If their roles had been reversed and he was facing his father, she would have bailed too.

Joseph waited until Jake was gone to answer her. "I just got back into town. I was on my way home from the airport. Julia thought it would be a good idea if I checked on you."

Thanks, Julia. This cemented her belief that quite possibly Julia and Joseph were made for each other after all. If nothing else, they both had lousy timing.

"She's a nice girl," Marisa said. "I hope you can manage to hang on to her."

"There's no need to pretend you approve to spare my feelings."

I don't give a rat's behind about your feelings, she wanted to shout but held her temper. "I'm not pretending. I really do like her."

"I'm glad to hear that. Because we were thinking, Julia and I, that it would be more appropriate if you stayed with us while your building is being repaired."

"Appropriate?" It took several seconds for the significance of his statement to sink in. "Oh wait, you mean, 'there goes that Donato tramp again, living with some guy, just like her mother.'"

"Marisa—"

"You're living with a teenybopper and you have the audacity to judge me?"

"Julia is my fiancée."

"And Jake is my best friend. If he were female would you still have a problem with me staying here? If he were a lawyer and not a lowly musician, would it be an issue?"

"I simply meant that you should be with family at a time like this." He sighed, his face softening. "I didn't come here to fight with you."

"I don't want to fight with you, either." She was so tense her jaw ached. He wasn't the enemy. He was nothing at all.

"Have you heard from your mother?"

It amazed her how easily he switched gears. "Yeah, I got a card last Christmas. She was living in Florida with some man named Hank."

"She doesn't know about the fire?"

"Doesn't know and wouldn't care. Now, if I had burned up with the building and she stood to inherit some money, that might pique her interest."

That one got him. He looked down at his shoes. "I'm sorry she wasn't a better mother."

"I'd have been happy if she were a mother at all."

"Marisa—"

"Don't worry, I'm not looking for pity. I accepted a long time ago that I'm stuck with two parents who didn't give a damn about me. I'm over it, so you can go home and stop pretending to care."

He glanced up at her, looking wounded. "You were never willing to let me in."

"Let you in? So what you're saying is, your lack of attention and total disregard for my feelings is somehow *my* fault?"

He straightened, puffing out his chest. "I never neglected my duties when it came to you."

"You sent checks," she said, cursing the waver in

her voice. She was not going to cry. She refused to shed a single tear. "Here's a news flash. Checks don't read you stories and tuck you into bed at night. Checks don't congratulate you when you've made the honor roll for the fourth straight semester. Checks don't take care of you while your mother is out all night doing God only knows what with some stranger she picked up in a bar. Jake, he took care of me. He's my only family, and I belong here with him."

Joseph backed toward the door. "I should go."

Typically, when he didn't like what he was hearing, he walked away. God forbid he admit he may have made a mistake or two. "Don't let me scare you off. We can sit down and reminisce, talk about all the good times we've had together. Oh, I forgot, we didn't have any, did we?"

"I hope we'll still see you at the wedding," he said, his hand on the doorknob. "It would mean a lot to Julia."

But it wouldn't mean anything to him, is what he was trying to say? Well, she *would* be there—for Julia. "I promised her I would come, and I will."

"If you need anything, call." He opened the door and started out, then he paused, looking back as if he wanted to say something. For a split second she thought he might tell her he loved her. She longed for it. But only for a second.

It didn't matter anyway, because he disappeared into the dark without a word, closing the door behind him.

Marisa snapped the dead bolt, feeling she'd gone ten rounds with a prizefighter. Confrontations with Joseph usually left her physically and emotionally tapped. One part of her wanted to sit down and cry, while another felt like punching the nearest wall. A third, smaller part just wanted to go to sleep and pretend she had normal parents.

Three's the charm, she thought, tossing the sofa cushions in a pile on the floor. She was about to pull the mattress out when she remembered Jake was hiding in the bedroom, waiting for the all clear.

She padded across the floor to his room. He sat in the dim glow of his bedside lamp propped up on his pillows, a hardback novel in his lap. When he noticed her standing there, he put the book aside.

"So, I'm a lowly musician?"

She smiled sheepishly. "Sorry about that."

"It's okay," he said, patting the bed beside him. "I'm feeling a little lowly these days."

She crawled across the mattress and curled up next to him. He reached over and brushed her hair back from her cheek. It was a simple gesture, but it settled her somehow.

"Did you hear everything?" she asked.

"Yeah. I guess it didn't go so well."

"I'd say it was pretty much a disaster. We just can't seem to be civil to each other."

"Neither one of you seemed to be trying all that hard."

She buried her face in the pillow. "Ugh! You're not going to lecture me, are you? I'm so not in the mood."

"Then it's probably not the best time to mention how sexy you look in my boxers."

"It was all I could find. You think Joseph noticed?"

"At this point, I don't think it matters." He dropped his book on the floor next to the bed and curled up beside her, face-to-face. "It might interest you to know that I'm not wearing any underwear."

"That's funny, because I'm wearing two pair." She

slipped the boxers down her legs and held them in front of his face.

He took them. "That wasn't exactly what I had in mind."

"Would you believe it if I said I have a headache?"

"I think I would." He brushed her hair back, leaning over to gently press his lips to her forehead. "You want me to get you an aspirin or something?"

"I'll get it myself. I only came in here to say good-night. I should probably sleep on the couch."

"Okay."

She wished he would put up at least a little resistance, but knew deep down it was better that he didn't. It was almost midnight. He would be celibate soon.

"I'll fix up the bed for you."

"That's okay, I'll do it," she said, dragging herself up.

"G'night."

She hesitated for a second, wondering if she should kiss him good-night, then decided against it. That was a little too personal.

And what she had almost done to him on the couch wasn't personal? Not if she didn't let it. But, if she didn't, was she somehow becoming her own worst nightmare? Was she becoming her mother after all?

No. She was different. She didn't hang out in bars picking up strange men. The mere idea repulsed her. These feelings she was having were reserved for Jake, and Jake alone.

Why did that revelation do little to console her?

Jake's light went out as she walked to the bathroom. She took two aspirin and brushed her teeth, then found a clean T-shirt in the laundry basket. In the living room, she pulled the mattress out, smoothed the sheets into place and fluffed her pillow. Standing back, she frowned. A bed had never looked so uninviting.

She wanted Jake. It was that simple. It wasn't about sex or physical attraction. She just wanted to feel his arms around her.

Turning out all of the lights, she tiptoed back to his room. Through the dim light peeking past the edges of the shades, she could see him lying on his side, facing the window. His breathing was slow and deep. Trying her best not to disturb him, she climbed into the opposite side of the bed and slipped under the covers.

Much better.

She shifted onto her side, leaving a safe distance between them, and hugged the pillow. Beside her, Jake stirred. He rolled over, curling up behind her, sliding his hand under her shirt to rest on her stomach.

Oh, yeah. This was *much* better.

''Hmm, I was hoping you would come back,'' he mumbled, burying his face in her hair.

Covering his hand with her own, she tried to imagine what life would be like when this ended. Would it really be so simple to just let go of this intimate companionship and go back to the way things had been before? Would a simple friendship be enough?

And if it wasn't, what did she plan to do about it?

Hot breath scalded her neck and shoulder. The rasp of beard stubble abraded her skin and warm hands gently cupped her breasts.

Yes.

Her eyes still closed, Marisa rolled toward the heat, pressed the length of her body against him.

Jake…?

She was still in Jake's bed, still with him. She knew

she shouldn't be touching him this way, shouldn't tempt herself, but she couldn't keep her hands from wandering up his back, across his chest.

Oh, yes.

She felt heavy and limp with lust. It was all so real, yet...

Somewhere in the corner of her subconscious mind, she realized she was still asleep. She was only dreaming she was touching Jake. This wasn't real, just a figment of her imagination.

And if it wasn't real...

She smoothed her hands over his skin, wandering lower, cupping the heat between his legs. His moans echoed in her mind as she stroked him. In her dream he was hard and hot.

Touch me.

She willed him to touch her and, like magic, he did. He filled her with his fingers, caressed her. She felt herself opening up to him, arching against his hand, and wondered absently if she was thrashing about on the mattress. Was she really making soft whimpering noises, or was it all in her head? It occurred to her to open her eyes, to wake herself, but she didn't want to wake up just yet. She didn't want the dream to end.

Make love to me, Jake.

She murmured the plea over and over, until she felt the weight of his body pressing down on her, felt him thrust deep, filling her.

Love me, please.

Love? She hadn't meant love—not real love. Or had she? She could lie to herself while she was awake, but in her dreams, the truth was impossible to deny. There was only one reason this was so different from anything she'd ever felt. She was in love with Jake. And she would love him forever, even if he could never love her back. She could tell him now, because this was a dream. In her dreams, she could pretend he loved her, too.

I love you, Jake.

She said it again and again. And a deep longing clenched her heart. If only he could love her back.

The dream became frenzied and disjointed after that. She comprehended only sweat-slicked skin and pulsing sensation. The way dreams often did, it seemed to go on all night, escalating higher and higher until she felt herself spinning out of control. When the first tremors of climax gripped her, she let herself sink under, her body awash with pure sensation that went on forever and ever.

This was too good, too real....

Her eyes snapped open.

Jake didn't disappear with the vestiges of sleep. He was there, on top of her. Inside of her.

Oh, no. The things she'd said to him...

She was still humming with the explosive aftershocks of her release when she felt Jake tense, heard a groan rip from his chest.

Collapsing into her arms, he settled against her in the dark. She lay there, feeling the thump of his heart beating, his breath against her skin, wondering what she had just done.

Twelve

"It was three."

Jake filled a cup with coffee and slid it across the counter to Marisa. "No, it was two."

"Look." She turned the list so he could see it. "The no-spending-the-night rule is history because we slept naked. I wasn't anywhere close to ovulating, that's two, and we weren't at my apartment. That's three."

"Oh yeah, I guess it is." He frowned, scratching his beard-roughened chin. "Well, the third one shouldn't count. We can't exactly make love at your place anymore. Can't we amend number three? Now we only make love here?"

She dropped her head in her hands. "We can't keep breaking the rules and amending them every time we do."

His eyebrow spiked up. "This coming from the woman who seduced me on the couch?"

"That was different—we didn't make love." But they had last night—in the purest sense of the word. Maybe that's why she was experiencing this sudden sense of panic. It hadn't been a sleep-induced sentiment. She was wide-awake and the feeling was no less intense. This was no longer "I love you as a friend" love. This was deep down, from the center of her soul "I'm in love with you" love. Maybe it had always been there, locked somewhere deep inside her heart, and was just now breaking free.

She'd poured her heart out all over the place last night. The memory still made her cringe. She could only hope that he hadn't heard, or wrote it off as mindless babbling, or temporary insanity.

"What do we have left?" He slid the list closer. "Number one, total honesty. No problem. Neither of us will break that. We never lie to each other. And number five, no sleeping with anyone else. I'm not planning on sleeping with anyone else. Are you?"

"Of course not."

"And seven, no self-gratification." He looked up at her, a devilish gleam in his eye. "Which we've already established applies only to me."

"Don't even look at me like that, I'm still mad at you about last night."

He pressed a hand to his chest. "Mad at me? Jeez, Marisa. You attacked me!"

"I was sleeping!"

"You were climbing all over me, saying 'touch me, Jake', 'make love to me, Jake.' What was I supposed to do?"

Don't forget, "I love you, Jake," she thought.

Maybe he hadn't heard after all. Or maybe he'd chosen to ignore it. "Regardless of whose fault it was, we can't let this happen again."

"Then, as much as I enjoy your company in my bed, it would be best if we slept alone from now on. We obviously can't be responsible for our actions while we're asleep."

Disappointment clawed at her gut, but she couldn't argue with his logic. After she was pregnant they wouldn't be sharing a bed. No reason not to break the habit now. "You're probably right."

"And after last night, I think we should have a hands-off rule until you ovulate. It's too easy to cross the line into territory where we shouldn't be."

He wanted to limit their encounters to one or two a month? Not only did he not love her, maybe he had no romantic feelings for her whatsoever. Maybe she'd only built things up in her mind and had herself convinced he really desired her. She'd seduced him on the couch, and then in his bed, and he probably hadn't even wanted her. He'd probably made love to her out of pity.

Even worse, maybe he had heard her confessions of love and this was his way of saying he wasn't interested.

She felt her breakfast rising in her throat.

"Anyway, I'm at my two-week mark. I'm celibate until your egg is done cooking." He grabbed the *Detroit News* off the table and pulled the sports section out. "By the way, Julia called while you were in the shower. She's stopping over this morning."

She was so not in the mood to see Julia. Perky, happy Julia who would no doubt sense her despair—because perky, happy people had radar for that sort of thing— and try to cheer her up. She didn't want to be cheered up. She wanted to crawl back into bed and wallow in self-pity for a while. A week or two should do it. A month tops. "Did she say why she's coming over?"

"She said something about your clothes."

There was a knock at the door, and Marisa put her coffee down, wondering how she could get rid of her quickly. "That's probably her. I'll get it."

She opened the door and nearly fell over when a mountain of plastic garment bags were launched into her arms.

"Sorry," Julia said, from under the pile. "I think I carried too much."

Together they stacked them on the couch. "Are these all of my clothes? So soon?"

"I'm a regular customer. He put a rush on the order." She looked over at Jake and smiled. "Hi, Jake."

He refolded the paper and put it down on the counter. "Hey, Julia. Are there any more in your car?"

She held out her keys. "Would you mind? It's the red Beamer down the block."

Jake took her keys and stopped by the door to put his sandals on. "I'll be right back."

"He's so cute," Julia said after he closed the door.

"Yeah, he is," Marisa agreed, surprised by how miserable she sounded. "How much do I owe you for the cleaning?"

"You don't. It's my treat."

"Julia, the insurance—"

"Please, let me do this for you. It would mean so much to me."

Julia looked as if she might bust out sobbing so Marisa caved. "Fine. Okay, you can pay it."

"Thank you. Even though technically I'll be your stepmother, I meant it when I said I want us to be friends."

She couldn't suppress an indignant snort. "That would be a first. Of course, the others really weren't around long enough for me to get attached to them."

Julia looked hurt. "This is different."

Sure. That's probably what they all thought. "For both your sakes, I hope you're right."

"I know what people think of me, the way they look at me. They think I'm marrying him for his money."

"You're not?" She slapped a hand over her mouth. Well, that sort of popped out unexpectedly.

"It's not about money." Julia sat on a stool by the counter. "The truth is, I have a lot more money than he does."

"You do?"

"I've always been in love with your father, since I was a little girl."

Which couldn't have been all that long ago.

"After my father died, Joey made sure my mother and I were okay. He would take us to dinner and the theater, and he spent holidays with us. He took care of us."

Marisa felt an unexpected twinge of jealousy. He'd never had time for his own child, yet he could so easily take on the responsibility of another man's family? It didn't really matter anymore, she reminded herself. That was better left in the past.

"Everyone thought Joey would marry my mother," she continued. "But they were never more than very good friends. I think she knew all along that I was in love with him, and she could tell he had feelings for me, too. He spent a lot of time fighting it, out of guilt, I think. But after I finished college—"

"Wait a minute, you finished college already?"

"Two years ago. I got my master's degree in art history from Princeton. I manage a gallery in Bloomfield Hills.''

Marisa sat on the stool opposite her. She'd graduated from *Princeton?* Which meant she probably wasn't as brainless as Marisa had assumed. She was getting the sneaking suspicion that she'd misjudged Julia. ''You look…younger.''

Julia laughed. ''It's a curse now, being engaged to a much older man, but I'm sure I'll save thousands on face-lifts some day.''

''Um, exactly how old are you?''

''I'm only a year younger than you. Because we were so close in age, I always felt a sort of kinship with you, and after seeing all of the pictures and things Joey kept with him—''

''What pictures?''

''You know, school photos and snapshots from when you were a baby. He always looked so proud when he showed them to people. I guess I was a little jealous.''

A lump formed in Marisa's throat. ''He was proud of me?''

''He was always talking about something you had done in school or how smart you were. He would carry pictures in his pocket that you had drawn, or copies of your report card.''

Marisa remembered sending him things—drawings, report cards, pictures. She sipped her coffee, hoping to wash away the rapidly expanding lump, only to find that it wouldn't go down.

''I always wanted to meet you,'' Julia continued. ''But he said that your mother made it difficult for him to visit. He didn't mean to be a bad father.''

''Please don't try to make excuses for him. It won't change things.''

"I think it's important for both of you to reconcile your differences—to build a real father-daughter relationship. So you can both move on."

Psychobabble, just what she needed. "Let me guess, you minored in psychology."

"Bachelor's degree."

Marisa almost dropped her cup. "You have *two* degrees?"

"I started college when I was sixteen."

"You're just full of surprises aren't you?"

"Look, I'm not trying to dazzle you with my intellect. I really do care."

"I believe that, and I appreciate what you're trying to do, but I don't think it will work. Joseph and I just don't get along."

"Now, more than ever, it's important that you try— that you become a part of our lives."

"Why is it so important?"

"Because you're going to be a big sister."

Marisa loved him.

When she was sleeping anyway, which Jake had decided didn't really count. People said all sorts of things in their sleep. Then they woke up.

Whether she'd meant it or not wasn't even the issue. He was the one dreaming if he thought he deserved her love, if he thought he had it in him to keep her and his baby happy.

As much as it pained him to put limitations on their friendship, pursuing a physical relationship outside of the baby-making process was unfair to them both. He'd had himself convinced that he would sleep with her a couple of times and get it out of his system. He'd honestly thought that years of adoration would just melt away and he wouldn't spend the rest of his life wishing things were different.

Adoration, my foot. He was in love with her. He'd been in love with her for the better part of seventeen years. That day in the fifth grade when she'd looked up at him, small and frightened and confused, he'd lost his heart forever.

Oh well, it was better off with her. It wasn't doing him much good, damaged as it was.

Fighting back an uncharacteristic surge of emotion— the kind he seemed to be feeling a lot lately—Jake popped the trunk on Julia's convertible BMW and grabbed the last of Marisa's clothes. He needed to keep himself busy today, and away from Marisa. If he hadn't already offered to let her stay with him, he would have suggested she stay with her father or Lucy. The more time they spent together, the harder it would be to keep his priorities in place.

Sleep with her a few times and get her out of his system? *Yeah, right.*

He started back up the street, battling the urge to make a quick stop in the party store for a pack of smokes. That would only be a temporary fix. The agonizing weeks of withdrawal he would suffer when he quit again would only make things worse.

A gust of wind snapped against the plastic garment bags, carrying with it the scent of a cool summer rain. To the south, a line of ominous black clouds bisected the morning sky and the deep baritone of thunder rumbled in the distance. There was a storm brewing—from the looks of it, a nasty one. At least the weather would complement his mood.

Balancing the clothes in one arm, he opened the front door. Marisa and Julia were in the kitchen.

"I am so sorry," Marisa was saying. She was on her knees, wiping up a what looked to be a puddle of coffee and the broken remains of a cup. "I hope that doesn't stain."

Julia sat on a stool, dabbing at a stain on the leg of her white pants. "I told you, it's not a big deal. I probably shouldn't have just blurted it out like that. I should have prepared you."

Marisa looked up at her. "Trust me, there was nothing that you could have said to prepare me for this."

Jake dropped the clothes on the couch with the others. "What happened in here?"

"I broke your cup," Marisa said. "Julia was just telling me that I'm going to be a sister."

"No kidding? Wow, congratulations." He looked from Marisa to Julia. "You, um, want some help with that?"

"No, I've got it." She wiped up the last of the mess and dumped the soiled paper towels and broken cup into the trash.

There was a brief, uncomfortable silence, then Julia stood. "I guess I should go now."

Marisa laid a hand on her arm. "Julia—"

"You don't have to say anything. I didn't expect you to unconditionally welcome me into your life. I know I have to build your trust. I'm prepared to do that."

Marisa walked her to the door. "Thanks for getting my clothes. And congratulations, I'm excited for you both."

She sounded sincere, but Jake could see the tension in her neck and shoulders. He was pretty sure she wasn't feeling at all excited about Julia's news.

Marisa closed the door behind her and fell against it.

She took a deep breath and blew it out. "That was enlightening."

Jake took a tentative step toward her. "Are you okay? I mean, this must bother you a little."

"A little? Jake, this bothers me on so many levels I don't know where to begin."

"Maybe if you—"

"I mean, what was he thinking? How can he have another child when he did such a lousy job with the one he's got? And think of the poor kid." Her voice rose in pitch with every word. "This baby is going to grow up fatherless, just like I did. Joseph will get tired of Julia then he'll leave her to raise the baby alone. How dare he bring another child into this world under those circumstances!"

Jake knew this probably wasn't the politically correct thing to say, but he couldn't stop himself. "Isn't that what you're doing? Your baby isn't going to have a father either."

She looked as if he'd slapped her.

He quickly backpedaled. "I'm not saying that what you're doing is a bad thing, Marisa. If I didn't think you would be a great single mother, I would have never agreed to father your child. I have one-hundred-percent confidence in you. If Joseph fails this baby for whatever reason, you don't know that Julia wouldn't do just as well on her own. And you don't know that Joseph will fail her. Maybe the thought of him being a good father hurts you even more."

"Julia wants me to patch things up with him."

"Maybe you should try. It couldn't hurt, right?"

"Actually, it could hurt a lot. I tried for years to get his attention and believe me when I say the rejection hurt. I'm not putting myself through that again." Tears welled in her eyes. "Not only that, but…but…"

"But, you wish it was you who was pregnant."

She nodded, fat tears spilling onto her cheeks. They rolled down her face and dripped off her chin, leaving wet dots on the front of her shirt. "It's not fair," she whispered. "What if I never get pregnant?"

He had promised himself he wouldn't touch her, but he couldn't stand there and watch her cry. Bridging the distance between them, he pulled her into his arms. She melted against him, a bundle of softness and warmth. It felt so right he ached inside. "It'll happen Marisa. We'll get you pregnant. No matter how long it takes, we won't give up."

And God help him, he would enjoy every minute of it.

She sniffled, looping her arms around his waist. "I don't deserve you, Jake."

She was right about that. She deserved so much better, but she was stuck with him for now.

Behind him, the shrill of the phone drowned out the sound of her soft sniffles.

Marisa gazed up at him. "Shouldn't you get that?"

Reluctantly he let her go, troubled by how empty he felt without her in his arms. Though it would be tough—hell, it would be torture—keeping his distance was the smartest thing to do right now. For both their sakes.

He grabbed the cordless off the counter in the kitchen. "Yeah."

"Jake, it's Louis. We need you at the studio, pronto."

"What's wrong?"

"It looks like Aaron finally made good on his threat."

Thirteen

—

Jake looked down at the shattered remains of the digital tapes, feeling curiously numb—unusual considering his life's work lay crushed on the studio floor. "Why weren't they in the vault?"

Tank huddled in the corner, looking amazingly small for a man his size. "I just went out for breakfast. I was gone twenty minutes, tops. No one else was here, the building was locked, I figured…" He shrugged.

He figured they would be safe for twenty minutes unattended in the studio. And they should have been. There was no way that he could have anticipated this, no way he could have guessed that Aaron would have the guts to break into the studio at seven in the morning, in broad daylight. Anyone who knew Tank knew he came to the studio at the crack of dawn and usually stepped out for breakfast. All they would have to do is wait for the right moment.

Tank looked miserable. "I don't know what to say, how to apologize."

"Don't say anything. We'll let the police deal with it."

"The hell I will," Louis sneered. "Did you see what he did to my equipment? I'm going to find that son of a—"

"No," Jake said calmly. "You're not. We're going to let the police handle it. The studio's insurance will pay for your equipment."

"And then what?" Louis asked. "We just do it all over? We start the CD from scratch?"

"No." He contemplated the hundreds of hours, the *thousands* of dollars he'd just lost. He kept waiting for the rage to set in, for his temper to flare, for the urge to slam his fist through into the nearest wall. Instead he felt numb.

"What do you mean, no?" Marisa said from behind him. "I won't let you give up."

She'd been so quiet since they had arrived at the studio, he'd almost forgotten she was there. Now, as he turned to her, he realized that she'd probably been too angry to speak. Her cheeks were stained deep red, her jaw was clenched so tight he expected to hear the crunch of her teeth crumbling and her eyes were two menacing slits.

Talk about rage. If anyone was going to be putting their fist through a wall, it would be her.

"I don't have a choice," he told her. "At least, not now. I don't have the money."

"Then you'll just have to find the money," she said.

"It'll take time. I have plenty of studio work, but—"

"My baby money," she said. "You can use my baby money to start over."

Louis and Tank exchanged curious glances.

Jake cringed inwardly. "Uh, Marisa—"

"It could take us years to get me pregnant. It would be an investment toward the baby's future."

"Maybe we should, um, leave you two alone," Tank said, backing toward the door, pulling Louis by the sleeve of his shirt. "Come on, Louis."

"Yeah," Louis agreed, though he looked as if he'd much rather stay.

"Well," Jake said, after they were gone. "There goes rule number six."

Marisa shook her head with frustration. "Forget about the stupid rules right now. And don't even try to tell me no. You're taking my money."

Jake crouched down, scooping up the mess on the floor and dumping it into the trash. The plastic was pulverized and the tape itself stretched and snapped and knotted beyond hope of restoration.

It was gone.

He should definitely be feeling something right now. Rage, regret, revulsion—*something*. He understood suddenly why Marisa had seemed so calm the other day as they gathered what was salvageable from the charred remains of her building. Nothing he could feel, nothing he could do, would make this go away. He could rant, he could punch walls, but it wouldn't accomplish a thing. In fact, it would probably make him feel worse.

Marisa hovered over him. "I'm not kidding Jake, I'm giving you the money."

"No," he said, "you're not."

"You can't stop me. If I have to, I'll steal your account number and deposit it in the bank myself."

"And I'll invest the money in an IRA or a CD, for the baby."

Marisa followed him down the hall and out the back door. "How can you be so...so...stubborn?"

"I probably learned it from you," he mumbled. He calmly shook the contents of the trash can into the Dumpster. The wind had picked up and charcoal clouds spit icy rain. "Besides, I'm not being stubborn. I'm being practical."

"You're being dumb."

He turned to her, sighing. "Marisa, even if I'm able to produce this CD, there's no telling if it will sell. It could be a total flop. There's a good chance I won't break even. Any financial advisor would tell you—"

"I don't have a financial advisor."

"Okay, if you *had* one, he would tell you that it's a risky investment."

"I'm willing to take that risk."

"I'm not." He reached for the doorknob, but she stepped in front of him. And she had the gall to call him stubborn? *Sheesh.* "Can we please discuss this inside?"

She backed against the door and spread her arms out, blocking him. Lightning flashed to the south and thunder rumbled ominously overhead. The spitting rain was turning into a full-fledged downpour now, but she didn't budge.

"Not until you agree to take the money," she said. "Or at least half of the money."

Rain began to seep through the fibers of his shirt. "We're both going to get soaked, and possibly zapped by lightning."

"Suppose your CD sells millions. What then?"

"That, of course, would be wonderful, but not likely. And to hope for it would be completely unrealistic." The shirt began to stick to his skin and rain leaked out of his hair, into his eyes. It wasn't like Marisa to be this demanding. Her behavior lately was at complete odds with her personality. She was suddenly so passionate and vibrant. He liked her this way, and at the same time the changes confused him. She was still sweet and gentle Marisa. She was just sweet and gentle Marisa with attitude.

Only, today that attitude was becoming annoying. In fact, it was ticking him off. "Move, Marisa."

"No." She pressed herself more firmly against the door. The front of her dress molded to her breasts and was becoming more transparent by the second. Her nipples were two dark, tight peaks under the drenched fabric. "Say you'll take the money."

It wouldn't take much effort to hoist her up over his shoulder and haul her inside, but honestly, he was enjoying the view. What was it about fighting with her that got him so hot? "You really want me to take the money?"

She rolled her eyes at him. "Duh? How could you tell?"

"Show me your breasts."

She blinked, then frowned. "I beg your pardon?"

He leaned against the Dumpster. "Unbutton you dress and show me your breasts. Then I'll consider taking your money." He knew she would never do it, though he had to wonder how he was going to get her back into the studio unnoticed. She looked like a contestant in a wet–T-shirt contest.

She looked up and down the back of the building. "Here?"

He shrugged. "Who's going to see you? Sane people stay *inside* the building during a thunderstorm."

She chewed her bottom lip. "You have to promise that if I do this you'll take the money."

What the hell, she would probably chicken out at the last minute anyway, and she looked unbelievably sexy soaking wet. He was definitely going to have to make love to her in the shower next time. "I promise to take enough money to replace the tapes Aaron smashed, and buy two weeks' worth of studio time. Fair enough?"

She looked up at him through long, dark lashes dotted with fat drops of rain. Idly she circled a finger over the top button. "You really promise."

"Cross my heart." She wouldn't, would she? Anyone could pull into the back lot, mere yards from where they stood. No, she was bluffing. She definitely wouldn't.

"Remember, you promised." She tugged the top button open, then the next, then the next, easing the fabric apart…

Okay, maybe she would.

He really had to stop underestimating her this way, or he would never make it through the next few weeks. Not celibate, anyhow. He had to tell her to stop. Right now.

Water poured down her face and neck, creating a river in the cleft of her cleavage.

He was going to tell her to stop. Very soon.

She unhooked the front clasp of her bra, peeling it away.

Now would be the perfect time to make her stop.

She slid her hands up over her breasts, cupping them, squeezing her nipples between her thumb and forefingers.

Jake, you are a dead man.

* * *

"And then what did he do?"

"He took me home."

Lucy gazed up at her from her perch on the edge of the tub. "And?"

"And nothing." Marisa studied her reflection. "He dropped me off here and drove back to the studio. Is this lipstick too red for me?"

"He drove away?"

"The lipstick, Luce?"

"The lipstick is perfect. Why did he just drive away?"

Good question. One that she had pondered to death the past two weeks. She still hadn't come up with a rational explanation. "Like I said, we have a new understanding. We don't touch each other. Ever. He doesn't talk to me much, either, or look at me. Or come home very often. He's been working every waking hour to make up the money he lost."

"He's in denial."

Marisa dropped the lipstick into her makeup case and reached for the garment bag on the back of the bathroom door. "No, I'm the one who was in denial. I let myself believe this was something it wasn't. After years of hearing how much he doesn't want a wife and kids, you would think I would have gotten it through my thick skull."

"Are you conceding that you would actually want to be someone's wife?"

"Maybe I would. Maybe if it was Jake I'd be spending the rest of my life with, marriage wouldn't be such a horrible thing after all." As if that would ever happen. She unzipped the bag and yanked the slinky black dress from the hanger. It was the first slinky thing she'd ever purchased in her life, not that Jake would notice. He'd gone far out of his way not to notice her lately.

"So, you're just going to give up?"

"Give up? I never had chance in the first place." Hanging her robe on the back of the bathroom door, she stepped into the dress, a sheath of black crushed satin that hugged the curves she'd learned to appreciate this past month. She no longer felt ashamed of her body, and in a small way, she had Jake to thank for that. If he hadn't agreed to this baby campaign, she might never have discovered the true meaning of making love. She would have gone on her entire life believing it was unpleasant and immoral. And because she had a body that her mother had coined as "built for sex," she would have deemed herself immoral as well.

"Zip me up?" She turned her back to Lucy and lifted her hair.

Lucy slid the zipper up and fastened the tiny hook at the top. "Why doesn't he, by the way?"

"Why doesn't he what?" She turned to examine her reflection. Not bad.

"Why doesn't he want a wife and kids?"

She turned to Lucy. "You know, I never actually asked him. I always figured it had to do with his childhood being so screwed up."

"Maybe you should ask. Maybe his reason is really stupid, like, he doesn't like nylons hanging to dry in the shower, or he doesn't want to share the remote control."

"Lucy, when a man adamantly insists he'll never get married and have a family, there's usually a pretty good reason."

There had to be a good reason, right? Until now,

she'd never thought to ask. It had just been a fact—a part of his personality.

Her reasons for staying single had always been pretty straightforward. She'd survived her mother's four hellish marriages and unending stream of sexual partners, albeit not without battle scars, and learned one very important lesson: storybook endings didn't happen in real life.

At least, she used to think they didn't. Now she wasn't so sure. She could definitely imagine herself living happily with Jake for the rest of her life, if he stopped acting like such a moron.

There was also the tiny problem of him not loving her.

"Whatever it is," Lucy said, rising from her perch on the tub, "you better hope it's not genetic, because you're going to be having the man's baby."

"Oh, shoot! I was supposed to do my ovulation test at noon." She looked at her watch. It was after two. If Jake didn't get home soon to change into his suit, they would be late for her father's wedding.

"You want me to give you some privacy?"

"I'm not really due to ovulate for a few days. I'm probably wasting my time. I suppose I should do it just in case."

Marisa completed the test, then finished dressing while Lucy watched the clock.

"Time's up," Lucy said. "What does it mean when you have two purple lines?"

Marisa's spun around. "What? You're joking, right?"

"No, I'm not joking, see for yourself."

Marisa snatched the wand off the edge of the sink.

Lucy was right. According to the test, she was ovulating.

Which meant more or less that she had to try to seduce a man who lately couldn't seem to stand being in the same room with her. Swell.

"You don't look too happy about this."

She tossed the test in the trash. "Luce, he's been avoiding me like the plague. Something is bugging him, I can tell. What if he changed his mind? What if he doesn't want to do it and he's afraid to tell me?"

"Ask him."

"You want to hear something completely crazy? I don't even know if I want to do this anymore. If having sex with Jake is going to affect our friendship, which lately it has, what's going to happen when I get pregnant, or when I have his baby? I thought we could both handle this, but now I'm not so sure."

"Marisa, for years now, all you've talked about is having a baby. If there were any way for me to get you pregnant, *I* would have sex with you! Don't give up now that you're so close."

She shook her head. "I just can't do it if it's going to ruin our friendship."

"You would sacrifice what could possibly be your only chance to have a child for the sake of your friendship with Jake?"

Would she?

Jake had no one else. She couldn't bear the thought of him being alone, of not being there for him. He needed her. Not in the way that she needed him, but his need was no less vital. "Yes. I guess I would."

"He doesn't deserve you."

"Probably not, but he's stuck with me."

From the other room, she heard the front door slam

and the sound of keys landing with a resounding clang on the kitchen table. A ripple of nerves tossed her stomach into turmoil. "He's here."

"Please have sex with him," Lucy pleaded. "Promise me."

Marisa hugged her. Only Lucy would make such an outlandish request. "I promise I'll give it serious thought."

Lucy embraced her, squeezing hard. "Be forewarned that if he ruins this for you, I'm going to have to hurt him. Badly."

Before Marisa could react to her threat—a threat she would no doubt carry out—Lucy turned and strutted out of the bathroom.

Jake stood at the kitchen table, sorting through the mail, glancing up when he heard them. "Hey, guys, what's up?"

He didn't look at them long enough to notice Marisa's dress, which didn't surprise Marisa in the least.

Lucy turned and looked at her questioningly and Marisa shrugged. She didn't understand it, either. It was as if she was invisible.

"You're late," Marisa said, dropping down on the couch.

"Sorry, I got held up in the studio. It'll only take me a minute to get dressed."

Lucy crossed the room and stopped right next to him. "Jake?"

"Huh?" He looked up from the letter in his hand.

She balled her fist, wound up and nailed him in the bicep with a quick jab.

"Ow!" Jake shrugged away, cradling his arm. "What the hell was that for?"

Lucy leaned in close to his face. "That was a warning. Next time I'll hurt you."

Jake watched in amazement as she stalked out, then he turned to Marisa. "What was that all about?"

Marisa shrugged, pulling herself up and heading for the bedroom to get her shoes. "She must be PMSing. You'd better get ready, we're going to be late." When he didn't answer she turned to him—only to find him looking at her.

Not just looking. He was devouring her with his eyes.

"Nice dress," he said, his voice low and husky. "I've never seen you wear anything so…"

"So?" she coaxed. *Come on, Jake. Give me something to work with here.*

Anything.

"I should get dressed," he said, walking abruptly past her to the bedroom, giving her an obscenely wide berth.

In that instant, something inside of her snapped.

"What is with you?" she shouted, following him. "Do I smell bad or something? Is it my breath? Am I so repulsive you can't stand to be within ten feet of me? *What did I do?*"

He cowered near the closet, looking as if he might hop in, shut the door and hide. "You didn't do anything. It's me."

"What's wrong with you?"

"I, uh, think we need to sit down and have a long talk."

"Now?" She checked her watch, dread burrowing into the pit of her stomach. Jake didn't do "long talks," so she was pretty sure that whatever it was they needed to talk about was bad. "We're running late. Why don't you get dressed and we'll talk on the way there."

Fourteen

Jake clutched the steering wheel with sweaty palms. The air-conditioning was blasting, but it felt as though they were riding in a mobile oven. She was going to hate him. He would be lucky if she ever spoke to him again after this. But he had no choice.

"Okay," she said, shifting in her seat to face him. "Spill it."

He tugged at the collar of his suit. The tie Marisa had fastened around his neck felt like a noose. And now she was asking him to hang himself with it. "I'm not quite sure where to start."

"I don't care where you start. Just *start*."

He took a deep breath. "You know the producer that's been hanging around the bar lately?"

She stared blankly. "Producer?"

"You know, the blonde that you thought I was dating." He looked over at Marisa, cautiously, so that his eyes didn't stray to her cleavage. That dress was something else. Now that he'd seen her in it, he couldn't stop thinking about how he might get her out of it.

"She's a producer? She looks more like a groupie."

"She is a producer—a good one."

A tiny wrinkle creased her brow. "Oh."

"You look confused."

"I'm just wondering what this has to do with you and me. Are you s-seeing her?"

"Seeing her?" He laughed. "No, I'm not seeing her. Her husband probably wouldn't approve."

"Then what—"

"I'm getting to that part." He braced his hands tighter on the wheel. "She booked me on a six-month jazz tour. It starts in New York and we'll work our way to California."

"Six months?"

He forced himself to look at her. "I know I promised you I would do this baby thing, but it's a huge tour. The money is fantastic. I'll make enough to take some time off and finish the CD."

"When are you leaving?" she asked softly.

"Tomorrow."

"*Tomorrow?*"

A volley of emotions passed across her face: anger, confusion, disappointment. And hurt. Damn, he didn't want to hurt her.

"And the money I gave you? What happened to that?"

"I invested it. For the baby."

"When did you plan on telling me all of this?" she asked.

"Soon." He should have told her the minute he found out, but he couldn't bear to see her so let down, to know he'd made her feel that way. "I was thinking that if we planned it right, maybe I can be here when you ovulate. Maybe I can fly home, even if it's just for a few hours."

"No. That would be insane. It would never work."

"But I promised. I've never broken a promise to you."

"It's okay, I can wait until you get back. You will be back, right?"

"Of course I will."

She turned toward the window, folding her hands in her lap. "So, we'll just try again then."

Jake reached over and curled his fingers around her hand. It was cold to the touch. "I'm sorry, Marisa. I feel awful for doing this. I know how much it means to you."

She turned to him, a strained smile making her look more pained than happy. "I understand."

"You don't hate me?"

"No, I don't hate you," she said, but she pulled her hand away.

Marisa stared out the window, but she didn't see the passing landscape. She knew it was foolish, but she couldn't get it out of her mind that she had somehow driven him away. She would never ask him to pass up this opportunity, not even for her baby campaign, but it didn't make her feel any less sick inside knowing he would be gone. There was so much to be said, and no time.

"You're welcome to stay at my place while I'm gone," he said. "For as long as you need to."

"Thanks."

"Hey, maybe by the time I come back, your building will be finished," he said, trying to sound cheerful.

It only made her feel hollow.

He reached over and took her hand again. "Marisa, please don't be miserable. I hate seeing you unhappy."

She turned to him, forcing a smile. "I'm not unhappy." More like, dying inside. Big difference.

"I was really hoping you would ovulate before I left so we might get one more chance."

The thought of him in her bed tonight, for no other reason than to do his duty, to fulfil a promise, made the empty space in her heart triple in size. If he was going to make love to her tonight, he would have to *want* to be there. She couldn't accept any less.

"I tested just before you got home," she said, knowing that she was about to break the big one—their number-one rule. "It was negative. I'm not ovulating."

It was a beautiful wedding.

It was small and intimate, the flowers were lovely, the food delicious and Julia looked so happy Marisa was sure she would burst. Joseph, typically not one to display his emotions, beamed at his new bride. Marisa had honestly never seen a newlywed couple looking happier, or more deeply in love.

And she had never felt more miserable in her life. It's not that she didn't feel they deserved their happiness. She wanted to see them happy, she just couldn't help but wonder when it would be her turn.

If it would *ever* be her turn.

"May I have this dance?"

Marisa looked up from her untouched dessert, surprised to see Joseph extending a hand toward her. He looked dashing in his tuxedo, but she would have expected no less.

"It's customary for the father of the bride to dance

with his daughter. In this case the roles are reversed, but it still seems appropriate.''

She glanced over toward the dessert table where Jake stood, speaking with Julia's mother. He'd taken off his jacket a while back and rolled his sleeves up to his elbows. It seemed a small piece of her heart chipped away each time she laid eyes on him.

As if he sensed her watching, his eyes locked on hers. He'd treated her with kid gloves all day, as if the slightest provocation would send her hurling into an emotional whirlpool.

Well, okay, maybe it would have. She wasn't feeling particularly stable knowing that when they went home he would be packing, and in the morning he would be climbing on a tour bus and disappearing for six months.

Jake smiled when he saw Joseph standing there, and nodded, as if to tell her he thought it would be a good idea. Joseph interpreted her hesitation as a rejection, and backed away, letting his hand drop to his side.

She stood abruptly and thrust out her own hand. She had promised Julia she would make an effort. Now was as good a time as any. And oddly enough, she *wanted* to try. What did she have to lose now? ''Yes, I'll dance with you.''

He smiled, and Marisa was slightly taken aback. She couldn't recall the last time he'd smiled at her. Nor could she remember a time she'd given him occasion to.

He slid his hand around hers and led her to the dance floor. He was large and solid—intimidating even—yet there was something inherently gentle as he took her in his arms. His presence was hauntingly familiar, though she had no recollection of him ever holding her this way in the past. He must have though, when she was little.

Maybe it was some deep-seated memory she'd kept locked away until now.

"It was a lovely wedding," she said.

Joseph gazed over the top of her head, taking in the celebration, pride glowing in his eyes. "I'd say it was my finest yet."

"Yet?"

He chuckled lightly at his faux pas. Until that very second she'd never figured him capable of chuckling. "And my last. I think five is my lucky number."

"She's very special. And I'm sure she'll be a wonderful mother. You must be excited."

"Just between you and me," he said, bowing his head and dropping his voice to a whisper. "I'm scared to death."

His honesty left her speechless for a second. Joseph admitting he had fears? She never would have believed it possible. "Why be scared? It's not like you haven't been through it before."

"Look at the bang-up job I did the first time around," he said, his tone edged with regret. His grip on her tightened. "How do you feel about us having a baby?"

"I'll admit I was a little surprised at first."

"A little? I seem to recall hearing about an incident with a coffee cup."

It was her turn to smile. "All right, more than a little. I've been an only child for twenty-seven years. I never expected that to change."

"Family is very important to Julia," he said. "It's important to me, too."

The song that had been playing ended and another began. Joseph gripped her hand a little tighter, as if he feared she might back away. She was in no hurry to put an end to the first civilized conversation they'd had since…well, she couldn't actually remember them ever having one before. This was uncharted territory.

"This isn't the first time we've danced," he said.

"It isn't?"

"You probably don't remember. You couldn't have been much older than three at the time. You decided you wanted to be a ballerina, so you were always dancing around the house. You would reach for my hands and step on my feet and I would dance you around the living room."

The thread that had been holding her on this side of an emotional meltdown stretched to its absolute limit. She had no clear memory of the years before the divorce, but something deep down told her it was true, that they'd been happy once. They'd had that father-daughter relationship she'd always longed for.

Was it was possible to recapture those days? After years of having no one but Jake, would she have a family again? God knows she could use one right now.

It felt so close, close enough to reach out and touch with the very tips of her fingers, and for the first time in years, she was no longer afraid. Maybe it was irrational and due to the festive atmosphere, but in the depths of her heart she believed Joseph wouldn't let her down this time.

"What do you know," he said. "We're not fighting."

"So we aren't."

"Maybe you could come over for dinner sometime and we could try not fighting there."

She smiled. "We could try that."

"You could bring Jake, if you'd like."

A sharp pang of loneliness pierced her heart. "Jake

is going on tour for six months. He's leaving tomorrow."

"Julia says he's very talented."

She nodded her agreement.

"She said that you two take care of each other."

Emotion gripped her heart. "Yes, we do."

"I'm glad you've had someone to watch out for you. Someone special."

Special? Jake had been more than special. At times, Jake had been her lifeline. He'd kept her grounded. Why, she wondered, did it feel as if that was slipping away?

Tears stung behind her eyes. She concentrated on one of the buttons on Joseph's shirt. She wouldn't let herself cry. Not here.

"After four failed marriages, I'd like to think I've learned a thing or two about relationships. I know I'm probably the last person you would want to confide in, but I'm here if you need me."

"Thank you," she said softly, her voice unsteady. "That means a lot to me."

"Does it really?"

She looked up, surprised by the pleading look in his eyes. For the first time in her life she felt as if he really cared—as if he loved her. "More than you can imagine," she said.

"I know this won't be easy, Marisa. We'll have to get to know each other slowly. Learn to trust each other." He squeezed her hand tightly. "Do you think you could ever learn to trust me?"

If she dared speak, dared utter a sound, she knew she would dissolve into tears. So she answered him the only way she knew how. She kicked off her right shoe, then the left, then she stepped carefully onto his feet.

He pulled her into his arms, and they danced.

Fifteen

———

The reception wound down around ten that evening after Julia and Joseph left for their honeymoon. Jake made idle chatter on the drive home and Marisa sat in the dark next to him, listening to the sound of his voice, thinking how much she would miss hearing it every day. Not that she'd been hearing it a lot lately. Still, there would be a void.

If only he could love her.

Oh, sure, he loved her, but as he'd established when they began this whole baby thing, he wasn't "in love" with her. Jake, it would seem, didn't fall "in love" with anyone.

And why was that? she couldn't help wondering.

When they got home she changed into her pajamas and curled up on the bed, watching him pack. The closet looked so empty with one side cleared out. He hadn't left yet, and already she felt alone. In many ways, he'd left weeks ago. In all the ways that mattered.

And why had he pulled away? Why this fear of intimacy?

"I have a question."

Jake looked up from the duffel bag he'd been stuffing his clothes into. "About what?"

"About you. Why don't you ever want to get married? Why don't you want kids?"

He looked puzzled. "Why do you want to know that?"

She rose up on her elbow. "I'm just curious. I've heard over and over how you'll never have a wife and kids, but you've never explained why. I want to know why."

He shrugged. "I guess it's not that I don't want it. It's just something that I can't have." He shoved the last of his boxers and socks in, then walked to the bathroom.

She rolled out of bed and followed him. "Why can't you?"

"I would think that's pretty obvious."

She leaned in the bathroom doorway. "Apparently it's not, because I haven't got the slightest clue."

He grabbed his shaving kit and a bottle of shampoo. "Look at my family."

"What about them?"

"*What about them?* Are you kidding? They're worthless. My old man was an abusive drunk, my brother is in prison." He slammed the medicine chest. "Are you seeing a pattern?"

"I guess I don't understand what that has to do with you getting married? Are you afraid no one would want to marry you?"

He sighed heavily, as if he couldn't believe she wasn't getting it. "My mother warned me umpteen times about our family curse. Her father was abusive, my father's father was abusive—it's in my blood. Why would I subject someone I loved enough to marry to a life like that? Why would I bring a kid into this world knowing I would be a rotten father?"

For a moment she was too stunned to utter a sound. She stood there with her mouth literally hanging open, until he looked up at her and said, "What?"

"Are you saying that you'll never get married and have children because you're cursed? And if you ever get married, you'll spontaneously become an alcoholic and start beating people up?"

He yanked the zipper on his bag. "That's about it."

What was it she had told Lucy? Jake must have a really good reason for not getting married? *This* was his really good reason? A family curse?

She followed him back to the bedroom, feeling cheated—and angry. Angry at his mother for filling his head with nonsense and having so little faith in him, angry at Jake for having so little faith in himself, and angry at herself for not asking sooner. Couldn't he see that he didn't have a violent bone in his body? Didn't he realize that he was nothing like his father and brother?

You're one to talk, she mused. Hadn't she gone on for years believing that because she looked like her mother, she was destined to be like her? Jake's patience, his faith in her, had helped her to come to terms with the truth. Didn't she owe him the same? If he would listen.

"Jake, did it ever occur to you, that if you inherited

this so-called curse, you could be passing it down to my child?''

"Of course I thought of that. It was a chance I was willing to take. I'm hoping the kid will be more like you.''

"Which is worse, alcoholism and abuse or sexual deviancy?''

"Marisa, you are not a sexual deviant.''

"My mother was.''

"That doesn't mean…'' He trailed off, the crease in his forehead sharpening.

"Doesn't mean what, Jake? It doesn't mean my children would be? Like father like son. Like mother like daughter, isn't that the way it goes?''

"You probably take after your father.''

"Did it ever occur to you that you might take after your mother?''

He didn't answer. She hadn't really expected him to.

"When was the last time you got good and sauced? I'm talking, fall down, stinking drunk.''

He shrugged, lifting his bag from the bed and tossing it on the floor by the door. "I don't remember.''

"I don't need exact dates. Just a rough estimate. Was it last night, last week?''

He mumbled something under his breath.

She leaned forward. "I'm sorry, I didn't catch that.''

"I said, it was the day of my mother's funeral.''

"How long ago was that?''

"You know when it was. You were there.''

"It was the summer before we started the eighth grade. So that was what, thirteen years ago?''

"So?''

So? Is that all he had to say?

Okay, this was going to be harder than she thought.

"I still remember how upset you were. I remember someone saying that if she'd gone in for regular doctor visits they may have caught the cancer early enough to save her. But she didn't like to go to the doctor, did she? There would be questions about all of the bruises, and the scars."

"He didn't let her go to the doctor," Jake said bitterly. "Not unless something was broken. And even then, sometimes he didn't."

"So, indirectly, your dad was responsible for her death, wasn't he?"

The anguish of that day registered deeply in his face, as if it were still fresh in his mind. "Not just her death. He ruined her life."

"You must have been angry."

"Yes, I was angry."

"Who did you beat up?"

His head shot up. "What?"

"You were drunk, you were angry, you must have beat someone up. Isn't that what you Carmichaels do? You must have beat lots of people up."

"You've made your point." He started toward the door but she stepped in his way.

She hadn't even begun to make her point. "I'd like to know, Jake. How many people have you beat up? Ten, twenty? Give me a number."

"This is stupid."

"Stupid or not, I really want to know. How many?"

"No one!" He threw his arms up in exasperation. "I've never beat anyone up, okay! When you have a family like mine, people don't mess with you. That doesn't mean I'm not capable of violence. What about that guy in the bar, the one you were dancing with? I wanted to kill him."

"Did you kill him, Jake? No, you pulled him off me. Big deal. I would have done a lot more damage planting my knee in his crotch."

"I have to finish packing," he said, but he didn't make any effort to get past her.

"So, make me move. Shove me out of the way."

"I wouldn't do that. I would never—" He blinked, surprised by his own words.

"Hurt me? Is that what you were going to say? You would never hurt me?"

He didn't answer.

She tried a different approach. "Do you remember what happened the day of your mother's funeral?"

He leaned against the dresser, bowing his head. "Not really."

"Do you remember coming to my house?"

"Vaguely."

"You were so drunk, I practically had to carry you. Which was no easy feat, believe me. You were at least a foot taller and out weighed me by a good thirty pounds.

"We went into my room and we sat on my bed for the longest time, not saying a word. Then do you remember what you did?"

Eyes to the floor, he shook his head.

"You lay down, all curled up with your head in my lap and cried. You cried and cried like your heart was breaking. When you fell asleep I lay down next to you. I held you all night, and in the morning—"

He held up a hand. "I remember the morning."

"I've never seen anyone puke that much. I can't say I blame you for never drinking again."

He finally looked up, meeting her eyes. "Why are you telling me this?"

"I did something else that night. Something I never told a soul. I kissed you."

He gave her a funny little half smile. "Really? Why?"

"Isn't that obvious? I knew you would never find out. It was safe. Haven't you noticed that I *always* play it safe?

"I kissed you while you were asleep because I was afraid of what your reaction would be if I ever had the guts to kiss you while you were conscious. For years I've refused to even try to build a relationship with my father for fear that he'll reject me. Forget marriage. Marriages take work, and suppose I failed. How would I live with that?

"I even let you believe that I was asleep when I told you I loved you, because I was terrified you wouldn't love me back."

She wasn't sure if the surprise on his face was a good or bad thing, because he didn't make a sound.

"I'm sick of playing it safe, Jake. I'm so sick of being afraid. These past weeks some horrible things have happened. I've been confused and lonely, but at least I'm letting myself feel something. For the first time I feel I'm living my life and not just watching the world pass by around me.

"And you want to hear something strange? My endometriosis hasn't been bothering me as much. I think I was bottling everything up inside and it was eating away at me, rotting me. Unconsciously, I think I was hoping a baby would fill some void in my life. Like, if I watched my child living and growing, I wouldn't have to. I could stay in that safe little place I'd carved out for myself. Now I want to change and grow with my child. I want to be everything my mother never was to me.''

Jake still didn't utter a sound. He just stood there, chewing on his bottom lip, digesting every word she said.

''Don't you want that, too? Don't you want the chance to prove you're better?'' She walked over to him, placing her hands on his shoulders. ''I'm not going to play it safe anymore, Jake. Maybe you can spend the rest of your life afraid of what might happen, but I can't live like that another minute. I'm in love with you, curse and all. And you have two choices. You can either accept that love and love me back, or you can let life pass you by. I can't wait around for you anymore.''

''Marisa, I…I just…'' He trailed off, eyes lowered to the floor.

His message couldn't have been clearer. He didn't love her, not the way she loved him. Her arms fell to her sides and she backed away. At least she'd had the courage to try.

He caught her arm. ''Where are you going?''

''I'm going to bed,'' she said, gently pulling free. They both needed some time alone, to think.

One thing she knew for sure—the only thing she knew—one way or another, things between them would never be the same.

Marisa lay in bed, waiting for the blissful nothingness of deep sleep to swallow her up. It didn't. She dozed fitfully, tossing and turning. Replaying the conversation she had with Jake over and over again in her head, wondering what she could have said differently. What would have made him change his mind?

This tour he was leaving for had nothing to do with

his career. He had enough work right here in town to earn back the money he'd lost. He was running away.

From her.

Sometime later—it could have been five minutes or five hours—she roused to feel the bed shift, and the warmth of Jake beside her. For a minute she wondered if he was real or a figment of her imagination.

She opened her eyes.

It wasn't an illusion. He was there, gazing down at her through the dark.

She rubbed the sleep from her eyes. "What time is it?"

"Late."

"What are you doing here?"

"I couldn't stay away." He smoothed her hair back from her face, searching her eyes. "I don't care if it's not the right time, or if it breaks any rules. I need to make love to you, Marisa. I need *you.*"

Those three little words changed everything. She needed this, too. She needed it as much as the air in her lungs and the blood in her veins.

She wove her arms around his neck, kissed him. He sighed, his body relaxing against her.

"I've missed you so much," he murmured, brushing his lips against her mouth, her chin, the curve of her throat. "You'll never know how hard it's been, sleeping a room away from you, knowing I couldn't touch you. I've wasted so much time."

"We have all night. A thousand nights."

"It's not enough. I should have spent *every* night with you. For the rest of my life, I should spend every night right here with you." His voice broke. He spread his fingers on her chest, over her heart. "This is where I belong."

"You've always been there." She reached up and touched his face, swore she could feel tears on his cheeks. He leaned into her hand, pressed a kiss to her palm.

"No matter what happens, no matter what I do, I need you to know that I love you, Marisa. I can hardly remember a time when I wasn't in love with you. You'll always be a part of me."

Her heart caught in her throat and tears welled behind her eyes. She wanted it to be true, but she was so afraid to believe it. "You don't have to say that to make me feel better."

"I've spent the last seventeen years lying to myself, but I can't deny what I've always known in my heart. I love you, Marisa. Let me stay with you tonight."

She could only nod.

He undressed her, then himself. He made love to her, slow and tender and bittersweet. They were two lost souls intertwining, fusing an indestructible bond. Soul mates. She fell asleep in his arms knowing that every word, every touch they'd shared that night would live in her heart forever. That he would live in her heart forever. He loved her and they would always be together.

And in the morning, when she woke, he was gone.

Sixteen

———

Marisa lay on the sofa bed staring blindly at the ceiling. The muffled sound of traffic outside, the occasional drip of the faucet in the kitchen only intensified the feeling of isolation, the loneliness. She felt hollowed out and empty.

Numb.

Jake's scent surrounded her—in the air, in the sheets. She still tasted him in her mouth, felt the brush of his hands across her skin. She wanted to lie there and bask in the last remnants of their final night together. But she had to get up, join the land of the living. Even if the better part of her had died when he walked out the door.

His leaving was the slap of reality that told her he would never change. No matter how desperately she tried to convince him otherwise, he would never believe he was good enough. He would forever be running from her, and she didn't have the heart left to chase him.

It was over.

She waited for the tears to come, for the stark pain to claw its way through her, but she felt nothing. Well, not nothing exactly. She did feel an odd tingly sensation low inside of her. Heat in the center of her belly. She lay very still, concentrating on the sensation. It was almost comforting.

That's when it dawned on her that she wasn't alone. Her hand automatically folded over her stomach. Jake hadn't left her completely. A small piece of him remained, growing inside of her.

And for the sake of Jake's child, if it really existed, she had to keep going. She would get through this. Alone.

She sat up and wrapped herself in the sheet. She planted her feet on the cool wood floor, took a step and promptly landed with a thunk on her hands and knees.

''What the—''

She gathered the sheet around her thighs, looked back to see what she'd tripped over.

Jake's duffel bag.

But that didn't make sense. Why would he leave without his things? Her mind scrambled to reconnect, to process what she was seeing. Then she heard the jingle of keys, the rattle of a doorknob. Her heart stopped beating for an instant, then resurged triple time.

The door swung open and Jake walked in.

In one hand he balanced a paper cup holder with two cups from the coffee house down the street, in the other he carried a bakery bag.

He kicked the door closed with his foot, turned and stopped abruptly when he saw her. ''Good morning. Why are you sitting on the floor?''

She stared at him openmouthed.

He set the items down on the table and walked over to her. "Are you okay?"

She looked down at his bag. "I—I tripped."

"Oh, sorry about that. I must have left it there when I got dressed." He hoisted the duffel onto the bed then extended a hand to help her up.

She only stared at it. "I woke up. You weren't here."

"We were out of coffee. And I got muffins." He waggled his fingers, coaxing her to take his hand. When she didn't, he frowned. "Are you sure you're okay?"

He'd only gone out for coffee?

She was too stunned to answer, to make her mouth work. Here she'd lain in bed for the better part of an hour thinking she'd lost him forever and he was just down the block?

She looked at the duffel bag, then back at Jake.

His hand dropped to his side. "You're surprised to see me, aren't you?"

She nodded feebly.

"You thought I went on the tour?"

Her head bobbled on her neck.

Jake lowered himself to his knees beside her and cupped her face in both hands, locked his eyes on hers. "I'm not going anywhere. You don't have to ever worry about that ever again. Understand?"

The gate on her emotions gave way and everything her body had refused to feel since she'd woken up alone surged forward. A sob stole up her throat, choking her.

Jake pulled her into his lap and held her. She looped her legs around him, feeling she just couldn't get close enough.

"Shh," he soothed, rubbing her back, combing his fingers through her hair as uncontrollable sobs shook through her. "It's okay."

"I th-thought it w-was o-over," she managed to squeak out and Jake held her tighter. She knew she was acting like a fool, but she couldn't stop crying.

"I'm still not entirely convinced I've got it in me to make you happy, but I'm going to try my damnedest." He cupped her face in his palms, kissed the tears from her cheeks. "I love you."

"I l-love you t-too," she hiccuped.

Tears flowed in a steady stream and he brushed them away with his thumbs. "I hope those are happy tears."

"Very happy. Life is good right now." She threw her arms around his neck and hugged him close, nearly bursting with joy. Jake was there, and he wasn't leaving. And quite possibly they were going to be a family soon.

Life was very, very good.

He rubbed his hands soothingly up her back and arms until the tears finally subsided. Marisa sighed against his shoulder, feeling she never wanted to let go.

The sheet she was wearing slipped down off her shoulders and Jake growled low in his throat. He skimmed his hands across her bare skin. "Are you naked under there?"

Pulling back to see his face, she grinned and nodded. The last of her tears dried in salty trails on her cheeks.

"I say we lock the door, turn off the phone and spend the rest of the day in bed celebrating."

She let the sheet drop, loving the hungry look in his eyes. "I say that's a great idea."

He lifted her off the floor and laid her gently across the bed, then he tore his shirt over his head, shoved his shorts off and dropped down next to her.

"What about the coffee?" she asked.

He nipped at her neck, nibbled her earlobe. "We'll get more later. Right now I want to kiss every inch of your…" He made a face, groaned and dropped his head to her shoulder. "Aw, hell."

"What's wrong?"

"We can't do this."

"Why not?"

"We're supposed to wait until you ovulate. I'm supposed to be celibate. I don't want to ruin our chances."

Emotion caught in her throat and she felt herself welling up again. Happy tears. "You still want to have a baby?"

"Marisa, I want it all. Marriage, kids, a house with a backyard and a swing set. The whole package. But if you want to wait until we're married, that's okay, too."

"Actually, I think it's a little late for that." A grin kicked up the corners of her mouth. "I think it may have already happened last night."

"But, how? You said you weren't ovulating."

"I lied to you. I'm sorry, but I didn't want you making love to me because you had to. I wanted it to be real."

"Oh, it was real." He rested his hand over her belly, his face filled with wonder. "There could be a part of me inside of you? Growing, right now?"

"The best part."

"God, I hope so." He took her hand, held it tight. "Just in case you are pregnant, let's not wait. Let's get married right away. I want to do this right."

Marisa sat up, her face serious. "I do, too, but before we make this official, there's something we have to do."

He didn't hesitate. "Anything you want, I'll do it."

"Ground rules," she said. "We need to establish some ground rules. You know, so things don't get confusing."

"Ground rules, huh?" He nodded thoughtfully, a slow smile spreading across his face. "That might not be a bad idea."

"Of course, we should start with total honesty."

"Of course," he agreed. "And no sleeping with anyone else."

"Obviously."

"And then there's making love. I think we should do it anywhere we want, every day."

"*Every* day?"

"At least. And we're going to make love in the shower." At her curious glance, he added, "Don't ask, just nod and agree with me."

She gave an obligatory nod. "I agree."

"And I'm going to tell you that I love you a thousand times a day, to make up for lost time." He caressed her belly softly. "And I'm going to be a good father, a good husband."

"I never doubted it." She curled her hand over his. "I do have one question, though."

"What's that?"

Her smile was devilishly playful, but full of love. "When do we get started?"

* * * * *

eHARLEQUIN.com

Your favorite authors are just a click away
at www.eHarlequin.com!

- Take our **Sister Author Quiz** and
  we'll match you up with the author
  most like you!

- Choose from over 500
  author **profiles!**

- Chat with your favorite authors
  on our **message boards.**

- Are you an author in the making?
  Get advice from published authors
  in **The Inside Scoop!**

- Get the latest on **author appearances**
  and tours!

*Want to know more about your
favorite romance authors?*

Choose from over 500 author profiles!

**Learn about your favorite authors
in a fun, interactive setting—
visit www.eHarlequin.com today!**

If you enjoyed what you just read,
then we've got an offer you can't resist!

Take 2 bestselling
love stories FREE!
Plus get a FREE surprise gift!

Clip this page and mail it to Silhouette Reader Service™

IN U.S.A.
3010 Walden Ave.
P.O. Box 1867
Buffalo, N.Y. 14240-1867

IN CANADA
P.O. Box 609
Fort Erie, Ontario
L2A 5X3

YES! Please send me 2 free Silhouette Desire® novels and my free surprise gift. After receiving them, if I don't wish to receive anymore, I can return the shipping statement marked cancel. If I don't cancel, I will receive 6 brand-new novels every month, before they're available in stores! In the U.S.A., bill me at the bargain price of $3.57 plus 25¢ shipping and handling per book and applicable sales tax, if any*. In Canada, bill me at the bargain price of $4.24 plus 25¢ shipping and handling per book and applicable taxes**. That's the complete price and a savings of at least 10% off the cover prices—what a great deal! I understand that accepting the 2 free books and gift places me under no obligation ever to buy any books. I can always return a shipment and cancel at any time. Even if I never buy another book from Silhouette, the 2 free books and gift are mine to keep forever.

225 SDN DNUP
326 SDN DNUQ

Name	(PLEASE PRINT)	
Address	Apt.#	
City	State/Prov.	Zip/Postal Code

* Terms and prices subject to change without notice. Sales tax applicable in N.Y.
** Canadian residents will be charged applicable provincial taxes and GST.
All orders subject to approval. Offer limited to one per household and not valid to current Silhouette Desire® subscribers.
® are registered trademarks of Harlequin Books S.A., used under license.

DES02   ©1998 Harlequin Enterprises Limited

DIXIE BROWNING

tantalizes readers with her latest
romance from Silhouette Desire:

Driven to Distraction
(Silhouette Desire #1568)

You'll feel the heat when a beautiful columnist
finds herself compelled by desire for a
long-legged lawman. Can close proximity
bring out their secret longings?

Available March 2004 at your favorite retail outlet.

COMING NEXT MONTH

#1567 SIN CITY WEDDING—Katherine Garbera
Dynasties: The Danforths
When ex-flame Larissa Nelson showed up on Jacob Danforth's doorstep with a child she claimed was his, the duty-bound billionaire demanded they marry. A quickie wedding in Vegas joined Jacob and the shy librarian in a marriage of convenience, but living as husband and wife stirred passions that neither could deny…nor resist.

#1568 DRIVEN TO DISTRACTION—Dixie Browning
An unofficial investigation led both Maggie Riley and Ben Hunter to sign up for a painting class. As artists, the advice columnist and ex-cop were complete failures, but as lovers they were *red-hot*. Soon the mystery they'd come to solve was taking a back seat to their unquenchable desires!

#1569 PRETENDING WITH THE PLAYBOY—Cathleen Galitz
Texas Cattleman's Club: The Stolen Baby
Outwardly charming, secretly cynical, Alexander Kent held no illusions about love. Then the former FBI agent was paired with prim and innocent Stephanie Firth on an undercover mission. Posing as a couple led to some heated moments. Too bad intense lovemaking wasn't enough to base forever on. Or was it?

#1570 PRIVATE INDISCRETIONS—Susan Crosby
Behind Closed Doors
Former bad boy Sam Remington returned to his hometown after fifteen years with only one thing in mind: Dana Sterling. The former golden girl turned U.S. Senator had been the stuff of fantasies for adolescent Sam…and still was. But when threats put Dana in danger, could Sam put his desires aside and save her?

#1571 A TEMPTING ENGAGEMENT—Bronwyn Jameson
He'd woken with a hangover—and a very naked nanny in his bed. Trouble was, single dad Mitch Goodwin couldn't remember what had happened the night before. And when Emily Warner left without a word, he *had* to lure her back. For his son's sake, of course. But keeping his hands off the innocently seductive Emily was harder than he imagined….

#1572 LIKE A HURRICANE—Roxanne St. Claire
Developer Quinn McGrath could always recognize a hot property. And sassy Nicole Whitaker was definitely that. Discovering that Nicole was blockading his business deal didn't faze him. They were adversaries in business—but it was pleasuring the voluptuous beauty that Quinn couldn't stop thinking about.

SDCNM0204